The Return of the Takeover PART 2

JT LEATH

Acknowledgements

First off! I want to Thank God for making this all possible. Damn I did it again (PT 2). Next, I want to give a shout out to my editor. My Family, my loved ones, and especially my beautiful Wife Sharika Shanta, for being here shining like the sun at night. And for the time and effort that she spent putting in sleepless nights typing and re-editing the whole book. This was definitely a journey trying to put this project together while going through the struggle. The only thing that matters now is we are here now and going to continue holding this urban book game down. It was not easy but God does not make any mistakes. To my son Aiden, Daddy loves you dearly and do not ever forget that. To my mother, grandmother, and R.T, yawl Rest in Peace and keep protecting from above. I miss yawl, and wish you were here to tell me how proud of me you are. I know you are smiling down on me; all I want to say is that I love you guys. Everybody who did not believe in me, I bet you do now!!! (PT 3) will be out soon, so be looking forward to it. To my readers yawl who I do it for, so thank you all and I hope you enjoy reading the Take over series. Real 2 Life Publications is on the move! Any writer looking to be signed, Please contact me. Jarvon.Leath@gmail.com (I.G JT LEATH (954)826-4093

Return of The Take Over PT2

It was a mystery how K pulled out of the coma the way he did; nobody would have thought that K-Dog would pull through in a million years after spending three-and-a-half years in a coma.

K-Dog decided to let Percy live after finding out he was responsible for putting him in the coma. K-Dog could have easily gotten Percy wacked after waking up and realizing that he was sleeping next to the enemy. Instead of sending him to his maker, K-Dog decided to make him a member of the Take Over family. Will K-Dog regret making Percy a member? Will Percy seek revenge after finding out K-Dog was responsible for killing his father? Or will Percy be loyal to K-Dog and the rest of the Take Over members? There's only one way to find out. Laying low (recap)

Killa
Chapter 1

Nobody has ever done it big and lasted longer in the city of Ft. Lauderdale like the Takeover Family. From the bottom emerging to the top, from nickel and diming to building a strong and powerful organization. They turned it into a dynasty. It all started with two young brothers from different bloodlines; both were loyal to one another with dreams of making it out of the ghetto. Many times, in black communities, young black males become accustomed to their environment; not knowing the path that leads to the life of crime is a system designed to trap you. Only a few individuals make it out and still become successful, while the other 95% fall off to the wayside. After experiencing the tragedy that comes along with the game, these two brothers from another mother who were from the five percent group to make it out alive.

The Fort Lauderdale Police Department had issued a warrant for Killa since catching him seemed impossible.

An officer on payroll brought to Killa's attention that the outstanding warrant concerned the death of Precious and White Boy Bruce. However, Killa wasn't hiding at all because he knew they didn't have anything on him that could make a case stick, let alone arrest him. Killa even turned himself in after staying under the radar for six months because his attorney informed him that running would only make matters worse.

11:45 AM

When Killa arrived at the police station, Detective Green was already waiting for him as he walked through the doors. Detective Green was the new head officer after the death of Graham and Brent, and he is just as big an asshole, only bigger. Everyone could see it, especially Killa and the other members of the Takeover Family. However, being the type of man Killa is, he just brushed it off.

"Mr. Keith Thomas, a.k.a Killa. It's nice to see you finally stopped by," Detective Green said, grabbing Killa by the arm. "This way, please," he said, leading Killa into a room to be frisked before they entered the interrogation room for questioning. Once they were seated, Detective Green pulled out a folder and slid it across the table to Killa.

"What's this?" Killa asked.

"Why don't you open it and see?" Detective Green responded, leaning back into his chair, observing Killa while he opened the folder.

Inside the folder were photos of Precious and White Boy Bruce with gunshots in their heads. The photos were very detailed.

"Do you know who's responsible for murdering them?"

Green asked while he looked for signs from Killa's body language that might give him away, but it was a lost cause because Killa gave him absolutely nothing.

"I'm sure you know by now that if I knew who killed my baby mama, they'd be dead already," Killa said in a reminding tone.

"So, you want to play games now?" Green said, walking over to Killa and placing his hand on the back of his neck. "Well, let me tell you something motherfucker! Word on the street is that your baby's mother tried to get you wacked, and it backfired on her and Bruce. Word is... you and that Goddamn motherfucker, Lil Coon were behind the triggers of the guns that killed them," Green said accusingly.

The entire police force wanted the whole Takeover Family off the street so badly that it irritated them just thinking of it. They wanted all them locked up for good, and they wouldn't rest until they brought their asses down.

"You know what, buddy," Detective Graham said through clenched teeth while pointing his finger in Killa's face, "this shit was business at first, but you motherfuckers made this shit personal. I will not sleep until I put you bastards behind bars for good!" He yelled.

No matter how hard Detective Graham and the rest of the law enforcers wanted to bring down the Take Over Family, they always seemed to be two steps ahead, and that's what they hated the most.

Hours later, Killa was walking out that bitch with his head held high; Bray was waiting when Killa exited the building. Killa walked towards Bray's vehicle and got in.

"What took so long?" Bray asked as she reached over, passing the blunt; she got the ashtray and gave it to him.

"You already know how them fucka's play," was all Killa

said before firing the blunt.

***

In the meantime, ever since K-Dog had pulled through, Killa was closer to him because not only were they best friends, but they both had experienced the same thing, almost dying.. Killa had a strong feeling that K-Dog knew who was responsible for almost taking his life. But why would K-Dog hold back this kind of information? It just wasn't adding up and making any sense at all. But Killa was going to make it his business to find out one way or another. And when he does, there will be a lot of crying, slow music, singing, and flowers.

While Killa was working at the car lot along with K-Dog, who was up and running like a brand-new car, Killa got up from his expensive mahogany desk after filing papers on a shipment that came in days ago. Killa walked towards K-Dog's office and overheard K-Dog's conversation as he spoke on the phone.

"Baby, yes, I'm sure he was responsible for putting me in a coma… I understand that, but he's just a kid who wanted to kill da person who took his father's life… you're right about dat, and I can never let Killa nor Lil Coon know about this. I am going to take this to the grave!" soon, K-Dog looked up; the first person was staring him in the eyes… Killa. By the look on his face, K-Dog knew he was busted and had some explaining to do, so the only thing to do was explain the situation.

"Bae, let me call you back… ok, I love you too," K-Dog ended the call.

"So, you weren't going to tell me, dawg… for real? After

all, we have been through?" Killa couldn't believe his right-hand man was holding out on him, but whatever it was, Killa wanted to know why. As for K-Dog, he knew he was stuck between a rock and a hard spot; deep down inside, K-Dog wanted to die and take it to the grave instead of informing Killa and Lil Coon.

K-Dog was sitting at his desk, thinking about the best he could explain the situation, knowing how badly the crew wanted to checkmate the responsible individuals.

K-Dog looked at Killa before saying, "Bruh, you got to promise me what I'm about to tell you; you can never let the rest of the members know. Especially Lil Coon!" Killa didn't like what he heard, not even for a second. However, he already knew that no matter what K-Dog's reasons were, he would have to respect them. He had no choice. So, Killa sat down in the chair across from K-Dog, waiting to hear every word. He didn't want to miss one single detail.

"Aight, bruh, I'm listening, so go on," said Killa.

Living good...Lil Coon
Chapter 2

Since meeting Shavon, Lil Coon has been thinking about settling down for the first time in his life. Nobody has ever made him feel like she did, especially in bed. The sex was mind-blowing. About two months ago, he opened a strip club on Broward Blvd. and 31st Ave. called The Dungeon. Thanks to Shavon, it was already up and running. She was the one who came up with the idea in the first place. The club was laid with black marble tile with real gold trimmings. The flat-screen TVs hung from the ceilings, and there were dancers' poles everywhere for the strippers to make it do what it does. Off the side of the stage was where the bar was kept and of course, it was run by Shavon.

Every day from 2:00 pm - 12:00 am, you could lay back, chill, smoke a blunt or two, or even catch a bad bitch. The Dungeon was the place to be. This was a power move Lil Coon made on his behalf. Not only was the club making money, but it also kept his focus in check. K-Dog and Killa had to give Lil Coon a thumbs up for a well-done job. Even though the strip club was a business place, it was the spot they chilled and hung out.

9:45 PM

Tonight, was like every other night. The club was jammed packed with strip club bandits. All the go-getters were in the building, making it rain. You had the Y. G.'s in one corner and the Monopoly Boyz in the other. Both cliques were filled with big-time scammers and check boys. You also had Major Playas in the building. They were in the dope game, so you know it was a lot of big shit popping off.

Tonight, was one of the nights where all the strippers walked around butt- ass naked trying to do what they do best, milking niggas out of their money. One stripper, Coco, was really doing the damn thing. She straight put on at the Y. G's table. Coco was built like a brick house, solid. She stood about 6'1 and weighed about 210 easily, but she was firm. Her body was shaped like a Coca-Cola bottle.

Jitt, the ringleader of the Monopoly Boyz, had a thing for Coco's fine ass. Every time Jitt came to party at Club Dungeon, he invited her to his table. Though, she did not mind being there anyway because the money was always good. Jitt was a young nigga who had big dreams of making it out of the ghetto like the rest of niggas who hustled with a motive. The only difference was that he had the remedy and blueprint for white-collared crimes.

When Jitt saw Coco shaking her ass like she was trying to make a baby at the Y. G's table, he felt some way nigga was mad, Coco knew there was static between the crews, but she did not give a damn! The only thing she worried about was dollar signs. Without thinking twice, Jitt got up from where he sat with his crew and walked to another badass stripper named China. He whispered something in her ear

11

and then walked back to his table. China was Chinese and Jamaican with long hair that hang down to the crack of her ass, so Jitt played his ace in the hole. Without hesitation, China stopped what she was doing and followed Jitt back to his table where he and his niggas was doing the damn thang.

Bottles of alcohol were being poured, money was flying in the air, and every member of the Monopoly Boyz had over 10k sitting in front of him at their tables. It did not take long before everybody noticed Jitt and his crew were doing the Y.G.s; all the attention was focused on the Monopoly Boyz. They were drawing so much attention that Coco stopped what she was doing and started looking in the direction where everybody else was, only to find China putting on.

How could Jitt play her like that, knowing they did not get along, let alone see eye to eye? Every chance Coco and China got, they were at each other throats like cats and dogs.

Coco made it her business to stop what she was doing, left, the money on the stage, and walked over to Jitt and his crew. Coco was heated straight 38 hot about the whole situation at hand; the only thing Coco saw was red in her eyes as she approached.

"Bitch what da fuck you doin with my peoples!?" Coco yelled out loud as she stood directly in front of China who was giving Jitt a slap dance of his life.

"Bitch what da fuck it look like hoe? I'm workin," China responded as she stood up, getting in her stand just in case a bitch got crazy.

"Workin!" Coco said, looking China dead in her eyes.

"Naw, ain't no workin round here bitch these, my peoples!" China yelled back.

China couldn't believe what she was hearing; she looked

at Coco with an expression on her face that said… I know dis bitch ain't tryna put down, let alone stop her from getting paid.

"Bitch get da fuck outta my face hoe, you trippin!" China said as she turned her back towards Coco and started back dancing.

Without thinking twice, Coco cocked back and swung on China, hitting her in the back of her head.

"Pow," was the sound that was heard as China fell right into Jitt's lap. Once China regained her composure, she jumped up, rushing Coco, swinging like a mad woman landing blow after blow. Coco was from the projects, so throwing down was right up her alley; they both stood toe to toe, throwing down like amateur boxers.

Titties, ass, and pussy were everywhere as they got down; niggas were throwing money straight, making it rain as China and Coco fought. The fight lasted for two minutes before the bouncers broke it up.

Shortly after breaking up the two, the bouncers escorted them to the back office, where Lil Coon was sitting back blowing purp.

"What da fuck goin on wit ya'll, and why ya'll always at each other throats?" Lil Coon asked. Coco and China were his best, top-of-the-line strippers when it came down to getting money; they both went beyond the limits. Lil Coon just couldn't figure out why they couldn't get along with one another.

"Dis bitch tryna take money outta my mouth knowin da Monopoly Boyz is my peoples," Coco said, looking over at China.

"I'ma tell you da problems; dis bitch think she owns and runs shit up in here. Listen here boo, dis is a business place. So, take yo petty ass home with yo washed up ass and find you somebody else to fuck wit, because I'm not da one." China yelled.

"Petty! Hoe, I'll show you petty" Coco tried to rush over to China, but the bouncers grabbed her.

"Let dat hoe go and watch what I do to her," China yelled!

All Lil Coon could do was watch through his blood-shot red eyes. He'd had enough and decided to take matters into his own hands. "Dee-Bo, let her go," Lil Coon said, "because if another punch is thrown up in dis bitch, both bitches gonna be jobless. I swear to God!" He looked at China and then at Coco. "Ya'll makin shit look bad with all that little girl shit, and If ya'll can't get along from this day forward, then find somewhere else to dance, I mean it!" he demanded.

Lil Coon knew China was dead ass right; however, he couldn't side with her or make it seem like he was going along with Coco's bullshit. "Now, get the fuck out and make me some money!" he said as he watched both girls exit his office.

"Bitch I'll catch you later," Coco said under her breath but loud enough for China to hear.

"Whatever!" China responded before going her separate way.

***

4th of July

Around this time of the year, Lil Coon always threw a block party. Tonight, shit would be a little different. Instead of throwing a block party, Lil Coon decided to rent a park in the hood so that parents could bring their kids to watch the fireworks. Food was being grilled for everyone, which of course, was free. Jam Pony Express was there putting it down. J-Dog rocked the mic as he deejayed, straight cranking shit up. Everyone was enjoying themselves as they did the City Boys dance. Only individuals from Lauderdale knew how to do the City Boys dance, but it later became known worldwide. You had all the youngsters getting their City Boy on, and Washington Park was off the chain. The old folks had their section where they were posted getting their drink on. I can honestly say the park was live!

Fireworks went off as everyone ate, drank, and got high as a kite. Out of the blue, some young kids around age 14 started chasing around the other kids with a Roman candle, shooting it at them. Just like that, a Roman candle fight started with the young versus the old.

Percy had become a member of the Take Over team shortly after he was discharged from the hospital. K-Dog made it his business to look out for him after they settled their differences. Percy was even allowed to shop in the hood on the other side of town. It was because K-Dog didn't want Lil Coon and Percy bumping heads.

Young Percy began doing his thang in Lauderhill off 55th Avenue in the Deva Hunt apartments. He was selling hard and soft, making mad cash. One day, Percy was sitting inside his trap, counting his money, when someone interrupted him by knocking on the back window. He got up and walked towards the window with his gun. He'd gotten caught slipping one time before, and he refused to let it happen again.

"Yea wuz up?" he said while looking through the peephole.

"Hey P, this is Pre."

"Ohhhh, Wuz gud Pre? What you doin in my neck of the woods?" he asked her.

Pre was a young girl around age 20 who had a great head on her shoulders. She was smart, educated, and kind of cute. She earned an Associate's degree in business administration after two years of college.

"Boy, I got some information about the person who shot u," Pre said under her breath.

"WHAT?" Percy couldn't believe what he was hearing. How in the fuck could she know anything about who was responsible for shooting him when he had not seen her in almost two-a-half years years? "Come to the back door," he said, still clutching his gun as he opened the door. "Come in," he said, stepping to the side so she could enter. When Pre came in, he closed and locked the door. Then, they both walked towards the living room where he had a 72 inch flat screen TV mounted on the wall. As they both took a seat, he immediately got to the point.

"I'm listenin," Percy said to Pre, who was too busy looking around at how extravagant the apartment was. Pre started explaining that a nigga named T-Boy was the one who robbed and shot him. She overheard him talking on the phone the other day when she was giving him a ride home. After he'd heard everything, Percy rolled up a blunt so that he could relax his mind. Pre had a thing for Percy, but his lifestyle made it difficult for her to get involved with him. However, that didn't stop her from lusting. Pre had to admit to herself that not only was he looking good enough to eat, but he also was coming up in the world. Just being alone with him was making her wet by second.

"You wanna hit this?" Percy asked, interrupting her train of thought. He didn't even know if she smoked or not.

"Yea, I guess," she responded.

So, Percy got up and passed her the blunt. Pre took it and hit it like she knew what she was doing but soon after, she started coughing.

"Damn, bae take yo time with this. This that loud pack, not no Reggie shit." Percy warned her.

Pre was coughing so hard that she thought she was about to die. The only reason she even agreed to smoke in the first place was that she wanted to conceal her thoughts growing louder and louder to the point that she assumed he heard them too. Of course, it didn't work, though. Besides, it was all in her mind anyway. Little did she know, the weed only enhanced her emotions, making her hornier than ever.

"Percy, what you had put in that weed, man? Shit got me horny as hell," she said jokingly. Even though she knew she was dead ass serious. She couldn't believe she had even said that out loud. The last time she hit a joint was six months before; she was still in college.

"What!" he said, surprised after realizing the words that had just come out of her mouth.

"I said, what you put in this weed because I'm high." Pre stated, hoping he didn't hear her correctly the first time. But it was too late; he had already caught on. "Pre listen, don't feel shame about how you feel because I feel the same way you do," he said. Percy had always wanted Pre to be comfortable when it came to expressing herself. It didn't take long for them to feel comfortable with each other. By the time they knew it, both were walking around butt-ass naked, getting their freak on.

***

Two weeks later, T-Boy, a Zoe from 8th Avenue off Sunrise, was racking up when he got word from another Haitian who hustled in the same area about Percy doing his thing. This Zoe was the one who had put him up on the lick with Percy in the first place. He told him everything he needed to know about Percy's new spot that he was trapping out of. After Percy did his homework, he found out where T-Boy was. Now all he had to do was execute, not knowing that he was laying on him too.

That evening, Percy was riding in a solo with his cousin Wade, and he devised a plan. Both men were already strapped with highly powered assault weapons. The trap that T-Boy was trapping out of was the first set of apartments, once you turned onto 8th Avenue off Sunrise. Eighth Avenue was a Haitian town because all the Zoes lived there.

Once he turned on 8th Avenue, Percy drove down the street to ensure everything was straight before parking behind the targeted set of apartments on the back street. He wasted no time as he jumped out wearing a monkey fit, an all-black outfit worn for scheming, and grabbed an A.K. out of the backseat. Wade also exited the vehicle wearing a similar fit with a mask. There wasn't a single soul out, nobody to witness the vicious brutality Percy was about to commit.

"Stay low, cuz, and keep your eyes and ears open," Percy said to Wade. Both of them stayed low as they proceeded to the back fence where T-Boy was. Thank God they didn't have to jump the fence because a hole was big enough for them to fit through. Minutes later, they stood behind T-Boy's window, looking through it to get a good view. They were surprised to see that he was there alone. They had to figure out a way to get in without alarming this nigga or setting off an alarm if he had one.

While Percy and Wade plotted on finding an entrance, a friend walked up and knocked on the front door. Within seconds, the door swung open. That was their cue to rush in. "Let's go," Percy said as he sprinted towards the door before T-Boy could close it. Percy snatched it back while laying both T-Boy and the friend down on the floor. "Go check the place out," Percy said to Wade before duct-taping them up.

Once everything was secure, Percy pulled off the ski mask revealing himself. It didn't matter if T-Boy saw his face because it'd be the last face he saw after tonight. "Wuz gud playboy? You remember me?" Percy asked angrily. T-Boy looked as if he had seen a ghost standing over him. "Search this shit while I beat the fuck outta this nigga," Percy said to Wade. Percy started kicking T-boy like he was trying to stomp a mud hole in his ass. Had it not been for Wade coming back into the living room with a safe, Percy would have stomped T-Boy to death.

"What the fuck! Nigga look at all this blood," Wade said in awe. Blood was every fucking where. They tried to open the safe, but it was locked.

"What's the code nigga," Percy , yelled at T-Boy. He only had to ask once because T-Boy didn't hesitate to give him the combination. Percy punched the code in, not realizing what was inside of it. Once he opened the safe, he found two bricks of cocaine inside, along with a large amount of money packed neatly in stacks. Once everything was taken out of the safe, Percy stood over T-Boy and shot him four times in the head. Then, he turned to the friend and killed him in an executional style.

Team us...K-Dog
Chapter 3

K-Dog was glad to be out of the hospital, but most of all, he was glad to be still alive and at home, where he belongs with his family. Dominique was happy to have K-Dog back by her side after almost losing him. Lil Javon and his baby sister were always in the presence of their father; wherever he went, they went too, and nothing felt better. As for the Boys and Girls Club, along with all the other businesses he dreamed about, everything was up and running. With K-Dog being the person he was, a mastermind with great intellect and business skills, he tried to put every one of his members in a position to run a legitimate business. All they had to do was listen and follow his instructions, and just like that, watch how their money would pile up.

9:45 PM

Ever since Lil Coon started up his club, that is where it seemed that he could always be found. Frankly, that's where he spent most of his time. K-Dog decided to swing by Lil Coon's establishment to check in with him to see how the club was coming along. Every time he entered that club, he became more impressed each time. There were still bad bitches walking around from every corner with their asses and titties out. He could see why people were always hanging out there. This strip club was liver than a bitch, and everyone knew it.

Once he fully took everything in, K-Dog sat at the bar where Shavon served drinks. It hadn't even been five minutes since he was seated before Venus spotted him and made her way toward him.

"Hey, daddy," she said while placing herself in the seat next to his.

"Wat's goin on sexy?" he responded, looking her up and down.

"Oh, nothing much, trying to get into whatever you got planned," she said, licking her lips so that his dick instantly aroused. Venus was trying to get some play, but tonight wasn't the night for it. Especially not with her. Homegirl was a shone. There wasn't anything that she wouldn't do for money. That's how she paid her bills.

"I just came to see what my dawg Lil Coon had going on," he told her, "But maybe next time."

"Okay then, daddy, if you need me, you know where to find me. By the way, they call me Venus," she said, getting up and shaking her fat ass in his face before walking away. All K-Dog could do was smirk and shake his head. He had to admit Lil Coon had some bad bitches up in this bitch. While K-Dog was looking around and observing his surroundings, Shavon walked up, looking as beautiful as ever.

"Hey, K-Dog," she greeted. "I see you met Venus already; what she got goin' on?" Shavon asked, looking in the direction she walked off in.

"You already know how things go in here," he said. "Bitches gotta eat too."   Shavon busts out laughing. "Boy, you crazy," she said, calming herself down. "Anyways, what are you drinking tonight?"

K-Dog thought about it for a minute before responding. "Let me get a double shot of Remy straight off the rock."

"Coming right up," she said before walking off to fix his drink.

Out of the blue, Percy came strolling through the doors with a couple of niggas from his side of town.

"Here you go, fam," Shavon said, passing him his drink.

"Thank you," K-Dog said, not taking his eyes off Percy as he made his way to the table off to the club's far side towards the back.

"Who is he?" Shavon asked when she noticed who K-Dog was staring at.

"Oh, that's just Percy," K-Dog replied while he took a sip of his liquor.

"Oh, ok, how do you know him? I've never seen him before."

"He's a new member," K-Dog said,

Shavon looked in his direction again, getting a better look at Percy. "What you said his name was again?" she asked questionably.

"Percy," K-Dog said.

Right then and there, at that very moment, it dawned on Shavon that she had a cousin named Percy that she hadn't seen in years. "Hold up right quick, fam! I'll be right back."

Shavon walked from behind the bar and rushed to where Percy was sitting.

"What the fuck?" K-Dog thought to himself when he saw Percy jump up and give Shavon a big hug.

22

Moments later, Shavon and Percy walked to K-Dog, paying them close attention.

"K-Dog, this is my cousin, and my first cousin at that!" she said.

"Ya'll kin, fam?" K-Dog asked Percy.

"Yea, man, my daddy, and her mama are sisters and brothers," Percy said.

K-Dog couldn't believe this shit he was hearing. With so many thoughts going through his head, all he could say was, "Well, I'll be damned!"

***

Two days later...

Since Percy was now a member of the Take Over family, he decided to introduce Percy to the rest of the members, including Lil Coon. It had to be about fifty members sitting at the table; K-Dog and Killa were also there.

Around 10:46 pm, K-Dog looked over at Lil Coon and Percy, who were staring each other down like two pit bulls.

"How is everybody doin tonight?" K-Dog said, hoping to defuse the tension between Lil Coon and Percy. Lil Coon knew Percy and Shavon were cousins, but he didn't like that Percy was a member and already had shit on lock. Truth be told, Lil Coon didn't have a problem with Percy, as long as he kept that shit on his side of the town.

"Now dat I have everybody's attention I would like to introduce you to our newest member... Percy, "K-Dog said, spreading his hands out towards Percy. Every member acknowledged Percy by nodding their heads and saying, "What's up."

The meeting lasted for an hour before K-Dog ended it

after getting everybody on the same page. Meanwhile, the crew smoked and chilled until a knock came from the front door; K-Dog got up and opened it, stepping to the side with both hands in the air. Four bad strippers stepped inside wearing police uniforms, pointing guns that weren't real.

The crew was looking at one another while the strippers approached.

"Ooooooh shit!" Percy said under his breath as one of the strippers came and straddled him.

Within minutes, all four strippers were out of their clothes, walking around butt-ass naked, giving the members a show of their lives. K-Dog had planned for this to go down the way it did, knowing it would ease the tension between Lil Coon and Percy. This was K-Dog's way of bringing them close together by simply using the power of pussy.

K-Dog was surprised to see Lil Coon and Percy chilling together, looking like two young bosses… mission completed. Like a true chess master, K-Dog calculated his steps carefully. Now it was time to take things to a whole nother level, but in the meantime, K-Dog sat back and watched as his plan unfolded before his very eyes.

***

K-Dog's bank account was doing numbers like crazy, already at $4.5 mil, just off the car lot alone. Not including the Boys and Girls Club or the pit bull kennel he started while Killa was locked up in Feds.

Like the true boss he was, K-Dog didn't have to risk getting his hands dirty anymore. Even though he was no longer selling keys, he kept it hood by letting the members push it, at their own cost… but of course, he still had their backs.

Members of The Take Over were not only selling drugs but also had small businesses as well. It was nothing to drive up the streets and see a place of business that belonged to The Take Over Family member. You thought you had Arabs setting up shop on every corner, but The Take Over Members were putting in work too, setting up shops right next to them, making it hard for them to breathe.

As for Sleep, he started a record label company and produced gangster music. The Take Over members weren't just about money, murder, and fucking bitches. You had to realize the type of caliber K-Dog and Killa were; they are the founders who started everything, from being on the corner to running the corners. There wasn't a place in Broward County the Take Over Family didn't have a business setup.

Giving Back...Killa
Chapter 4

Killa changed his name from Killa to Yashua. Yashua, who was transforming his community, opened a park for the kids to attend after school; if they needed help with homework, tutors were faithfully there. . Many types of programs were being funded for the kids to attend.

Killa also started a boxing program for anybody who was interested; it didn't make manner if you were a male or a female, old or young; if you wanted to learn how to box, then the gym was the place to be.

Killa even started a football and basketball team known as the Road Runners. On weekends, the players who played for the Road Runners would compete with other teams, from Miami to Palm Beach. This was a positive move on Killa's behalf; even the parents were glad because not only did they not have to pay, but if the kids took their sport seriously and advanced, Killa was gonna push them on a whole no-ther professional level… shiddd…it wasn't anything money couldn't buy.

***

Since the death of Precious and White Boy Bruce, Detective Graham was trying to build up a strong case on Killa.

He wasn't just trying to bring down Killa; Detective Graham wanted to bring down every member affiliated with the Take Over Organization. This cracker was deeply involved in bringing Killa down because he went far beyond the limits of killing White Boy Bruce, Detective Graham's nephew. Now it became personal instead of business because deep down inside, Detective Graham knew Killa was responsible for killing White Boy Bruce. Killa was always on point, two steps ahead of them cocksuckers, which they hated the most, being outsmarted by a black man.

The Take Over members weren't just anybody running around trying to make a name for themselves. They were real muthafuckas straight from streets who would bust your head just for looking at them the wrong way. The city respected them like they were gods, not because they were killers, but because they were living legends who gave back to the communities.

Even though Killa wasn't any longer involved in selling drugs, Detective Graham knew that Killa, K-Dog, and Lil Coon were responsible for the crime in the cold streets of Fort Lauderdale. And he wasn't gonna sleep until he brought the whole Take Over Organization down.

***

For some odd reason, Bray was feeling sick; lately, all she had been doing was throwing up. Her period was supposed to come on weeks ago,but it hadn't. The first thought that came to Bray's mind was pregnancy. But how could it be when getting pregnant was impossible? Since birth Bray was diagnosed with a birth effect that wouldn't allow her to bear kids. Had God found favor on her by answering Bray's prayers? She just had to know.

Bray decided to go to C.V.S. and get the most expensive pregnancy test money could buy. After Bray purchased the pregnancy test, she drove straight home, running inside the house like she was Ricky Williams, who played for the Miami Dolphins, nearly knocking Killa down as she rushed towards the bathroom.

The first test came back positive; then the second one returned positive. Bray couldn't believe she was pregnant; she cried for twenty minutes, thanking the man above for her many blessings. Bray walked out of the bathroom, making her way to where Killa was and sat next to him. Bray looked at Killa without saying a word staring him down; Killa felt something wasn't right with his baby.

"Wuz up bae is er'thang alright?" Killa asked, noticing the redness in her eyes.

"Yes, sweetie," Bray said, smiling. "Keith, I'm pregnant."

"Pregnant!" Killa said with that look on his face.

"I thought you couldn't have…"

"Babies? yeah, I know," Bray said, cutting Killa off in mid-sentence.

"Are you sho?" Killa asked looking confused.

"Yes, baby, I'm a hundred percent positive" at that very moment, Killa got down on his knees, spread his hands towards the sky, and said a silent prayer before resting his head on Bray's lap.

"I love you, baby."

"I love you too, Keith."

***

Days later…
Killa decided to hit up Lil Coon's club with K-Dog for

a celebration. He would soon be a father, and the only place to celebrate it was Lil Coon's club. The two pulled up in a Bentley truck sitting on 34s, looking like true bosses. Everybody, who was standing in line waiting to enter, was amazed as K-Dog and Killa got out, both draped in tailor-made, expensive ass suits.

The club was so packed that everyone was damn near shoulder to shoulder, and people could hardly breathe. Still, they enjoyed themselves and danced and partied to the booming ass music. All the strippers made their way over to where they were sitting, hoping they would luck up tonight. As Killa and K-Dog got their party on, Shavon brought them each a bottle of V.S.O.P Remy.

"Hey ya'll," Shavon said as she placed the bottles down.

"Wuz gud Shavon?" K-Dog said.

"I'm gud... is there anything else I can get ya'll?"

"Yeah! Bring me ten thousand in ones," Killa said, pulling out a bunch of $100 bills and handing them to her.

"I'll be right back," Shavon said while grabbing the money and heading to the back where Lil Coon was.

Moments later, Lil Coon came out with the money and made his way to their table. "Ya'll doing it big tonight I see," he said walking up and giving his homies some dap.

"I just thought I'd come out and spread some love; you know, support the naked hustle," Killa responded.

"Heyyy, I can dig it, I can dig it." Lil Coon replied. "But aye... Check this out; I got these new bitches I want ya'll to see."

"Are they bad?" Killa asked.

"Bad?" Lil Coon said, surprised that he even asked that question in the first place. "Nigga these some top-of-the-line bitches," he said laughing.

"Go get em then, bruh, let me see what you workin with pimpin," K-Dog said while looking in the direction where China was.

"Okay big bruh, I'll be right back," Lil Coon said, walking off. In no time, he returned with two beautiful bad bitches. "Dis is Season," pointing at the slim one with so much ass it seemed as if she was carrying the whole world in her pants. "And this one is Cinnamon," he said, pointing to the thick one with gorgeous ebony skin. Both women were foreign and very exotic looking. K-Dog and Killa looked at Lil Coon like where the fuck did he find these bitches.

"How ya'll ladies doing?" K-Dog asked, looking the thick one up and down with a seductive smile.

"Hello, papi," the girls said in unison.

"The only thing about these two is that they don't speak no English, but they understand well," Lil Coon told his dawgs.

"Ya'll have a seat," K-Dog said, grabbing hold of Cinnamon. K-Dog had a thing for thicker women, especially if the thickness was in all the right places.

"If ya'll need anything, just holla. I'll be in the back," Lil Coon said.

"Aight, holla, we got ya," Killa said while looking over at Season with her fine ass.

Lil Coon walked off, leaving the girls behind, knowing they were in good hands. Cinnamon and Season wore regular clothes, which was a good impression because they both dressed nicely. It didn't take long for the ladies to know they were in the presence of some powerful boss niggas. It became obvious because every time someone passed by, they acknowledged them with the utmost respect.

Meanwhile, while they all enjoyed each other's company,

China walked up and started winding her hips to the music. K-Dog grabbed some dollar bills off the table and gave them to Cinnamon. "Make it rain, baby," he said to her. She didn't have to think twice about it. She immediately started throwing money in the air and letting it fall on China. Cinnamon had never thrown money at anyone before, but she liked the feeling. Killa wanted to make the stake even, so he went and got Coco and made Season throw some money. Even though Coco didn't like China, she had to admit that she was bad as fuck too. Killa didn't know that Coco and China had beef, and they were at each other's throats every chance they got.

While everybody was hitting it off just fine, K-Dog and Killa just sat back and watched as two of the girls threw money, and the other two danced. As China was making her ass jump one cheek at a time, Coco was getting turned on from just watching China do her thang. Coco got in front of China and started dancing on her as if she was one of the niggas who threw money at them every night. China knew by the look in her eyes that Coco was feeling her. For a moment, both strippers began to feel the heat from that spark you get when being caught up in the moment. The chemistry was so strong that both strippers started tonguing each other down.

Nov: 2
Birthday Bash...Lil Coon
Chapter 5

Ever since Lil Coon opened the club up, body rates had gone down a lot. Niggas started hanging back on the street corners as it wasn't dangerous grounds. God must've found favor and breathed the breath of life into Lil Coon because Lord knows he was making it hard for them.

Today was Lil Coon birthday, and he decided to have his party at the Voodoo Lounge on Las Olas. Lil Boosie and Webbie, along with the rest of the Trill Fam, were gonna be there; this was the talk of the city.

One Stop gas station was packed with all kinds of vehicles from old school to foreign; everybody was chilling and vibing good vibes. Smoke was heavy in the air; music was blasting from damn near every vehicle parked at the gas station.

Around 11:45 pm, everybody started jumping in their tricked -out vehicles and pulling out the gas station. About fifty vehicles or more swerved from one lane to another, not giving a damn about the police.

Twenty minutes later, Lil Coon and Percy pulled up to

Las Olas in his drop-top Bentley. K-Dog and Killa were riding in K-Dog's Bentley truck sitting on 34's. Th Sleep, of course, was riding in his Lambo, looking like a unicorn in traffic.

Once the Take Over Family parked, they all exited their vehicles looking like rock stars; everybody was staring at them as they made their way towards the club. They all entered one at a time; as for the Monopoly Boyz and the Y.G.'s, they could not enter the Voodoo Lounge without being searched, regardless of if they were some getting money ass niggas.

As soon as The Take Over members entered the club, all eyes were on them as usual. Bitches were approaching from every angle, hoping to catch a bite. There were also hood niggas giving them dap and showing love.

Once the Take Over members finished hollering at the hood niggas and hood bitches, they started making their way towards the V.I.P. section, which of course, was reserved for them.

It didn't take long for the bottles to start popping and the loud smoke to fill their lungs; everybody was vibing. You had bad bitches on deck willing to do whatever it took to get a piece of the action.

The V.I.P. section was on the second floor positioned directly above the stage where the performers were taking place. It didn't take long before Lil Boosie and the rest of the Trill Fam hit the stage. Bitches started going crazy when Webbie came on stage with his shirt off, acting a fool. When Lil Boosie came out draped in diamonds, everybody started acting like the donkey.

Trill Fam was doing their thang, playing song after song until Lil Boosie called Lil Coon on stage out of the blue. Lil Coon looked at Percy shaking his head.

"Come on bruh... nigga let's vibe...you ready?" Lil Boosie asked.

Percy looked back at him then on the stage; Percy's eyes lit up like disco balls.

"Hell yeah, Fam, let's do dis!" Lil Coon yelled.

Right before the two hit the stage, looking like two young millionaires, Lil Boosie made the DJ stop the music.

"I got to a special shout out I wanna give to da birthday boy," Lil Boosie said as he looked over at Lil Coon.

"Happy birthday, homie,"Lil Boosie exclaimed and gave him a big ass bottle.

"Now ya'll need to make some muthafukin noise before we shoot dis bitch up!" The whole club started going crazy, bitches were throwing panties and their thongs on stage.

Seconds later, Lil Boosie walked up to Lil Coon while he performed his song.

"If you love ya nigga hug ya nigga and look ya nigga in da eyes and tell ya nigga you love ya nigga." At that very moment when Lil Boosie stopped talking, the deejay turned on "Yeah I love my Nigga" by Lil Boosie, and the whole club started going bananas.

While Coon was doing his thang vibing on stage, Percy was standing off to the side vibing to himself, keeping his eyes open. I guess the alcohol Lil Coon was drinking had to make him use the restroom; Lil Coon walked over to Percy and whispered something into his ear before walking off the stage.

Percy examined the crowd as Lil Coon walked towards the restroom seconds later. Then he saw some nigga who entered behind Lil Coon, but how he acted made Percy go and check it out; Percy knew something wasn't right.

Lil Coon walked inside the restroom without a care in the world, not thinking death was right the corner. He walked up to the second urinal and started pissing, not noticing the dude easing in behind him until he pulled out his gun and placed it to Lil Coon's temple.

Lil Coon got caught slipping with his pants down.

"Shit!" Lil Coon said to himself.

"Yeah, wuz up now, birthday boy?...I should blow yo head off yo shoulders," the gunman said as he applied pressure, pushing the gun harder to Lil Coon's temple.

"As a matter of fact, empty out yo pockets and give me dis jewelry," the gunman said while checking Lil Coon for weapons, which of course, were strapped.

The dude, who was robbing Lil Coon, was the same nigga whose car Lil Coon shot up at 1stop. Lil Coon knew he got caught slipping, but that didn't stop him from talking cash shit.

When Percy reached the restroom, he eased open the door, and right before his very eyes, he saw Lil Coon getting robbed. Percy pulled his 45 Desert Eagle from his waistband without thinking twice and crept inside.

"You think shit, sweet bitch ass nigga," Percy said before pulling the trigger, shooting his brains outta his head.

"What da fuck!" Lil Coon said as he was covered in blood.

Percy didn't stop thinking that maybe if he had shot the dude while he had his gun pointed to Lil Coon's head, he would've also killed Lil Coon. .

"Grab yo shit nigga, and let's go!" Percy demanded.

Lil Coon didn't waste any time as he removed everything

the dude had taken before following Percy out the door. Everybody was still partying like nothing had happened as they headed back towards the V.I.P section.

Once entering the V.I.P room, K-Dog knew something wasn't right; blood was all over Lil Coons' shirt. They both approached K-Dog, sitting next to Killa, and gave him the rundown. At that very moment, people started hollering and running.

That was the cue for them to get up out of that bitch. The Take Over members didn't waste time following suit; they all rushed and exited the V.I.P room with their guns drawn.

Once exiting the club, they all got into their vehicles and burned rubber, leaving a bunch of smoke behind.

Get it while it's good...Percy
Chapter 6

Ever since Percy knocked off ole boy, Lil Coon has been rocking with him heavily, especially regarding doing business together. Lil Coon was definitely looking out for Percy in a major way, giving him bricks on bricks at a time. Percy's trap was jumping like M.J. at the gym.

Instead of dealing with smokers, Percy stepped his game up and started selling weight ,In less than six months, Percy profited over $500k, which was in his safe.

One thing about the game is that when it came to selling drugs, you must get it while it's good because, in the blink of an eye, shit could go sour. But Percy had a plan, and he wasn't gonna rest until his mission was completed. He just had to wait for the perfect time to execute.

Today was Friday, and Percy's trap was doing numbers; the trap door was coming off the hinges by how many times it was opening and closing. Niggas were coming and going like the trap house was a pussy house instead of a dope spot.

Percy's next-door neighbor had to get on board after seeing what Percy had going on. Ms. Percy was an old lady who loved to smoke hydro and talk shit; her job was to sit on her porch and to watch out for anything that didn't look right, and just like that, she got paid a grand a day.

It was 10:45 pm, and Percy and Wade were sitting in the trap kitchen when a knock came from the front door; without getting up, Percy grabbed the remote control and hit a button. The 72-inch flat-screen displayed Pre was at the door.

"Cuz open the door for Pre right quick for me," Percy demanded.

"Aight," Wade responded as he got up, walked towards the front door, and opened it.

"Hey, big head," Wade said, stepping to the side for Pre to enter.

"Wade," Pre said as she walked in.

Pre walked over to where Percy was and kissed him on the lips.

"Hey sweetie, what are you doing?" Pre asked, sitting next to Percy.

"Tryna get this money, right?"

Pre sat at the table admiring how fine Percy looked while counting money.

"Damn, he looks so fine," Pre thought to herself as she became turned on just by looking at him. Between Pre's legs became so moist that her panties were soaked. The only thing on Pre's mind was giving Percy some pussy.

"Bae, can we go into the room?" Pre asked.

"Yea," Percy responded, already knowing what was on her mind. After counting the money, Percy stood up, grabbed Pre's hand, and led her down the hall to his bedroom. As soon they entered the bedroom, Pre pushed Percy down onto his king-size bed, making him fall on his back.

Without hesitation, Pre stripped down until she was completely naked and climbed on top of Percy.

***

Next morning…

While Percy and Pre were sleeping, Wade decided to walk to the store, which was only around the corner, to get a pack of backwoods.

Ten minutes later, as Wade walked up to the store, niggas were posted up getting their hustle on. Wade spoke to a few of them as he walked inside the store.

"I don't know why y'all speaking to dat nigga he didn't fuck with us like dat," one of the hustlers said out loud. "He's da reason why we ain't eating. Those niggas making all da got damn money." Homeboy was ferocious and mad as hell because he wasn't making the amount of money they were.

After Wade purchased the pack of Backwoods, he walked out and stepped towards the dude who was talking shit and got all up in his face.

"Nigga you know me?" Wade asked, looking him dead in the eyes.

"Naw…not really." He responded, looking around because Wade had him feeling uncomfortable. Wade wanted to make an example out of his ass. He looked around, making sure the police wasn't lurking before punching him dead on the bottom of his chin, knocking him completely out.

Shortly after, Wade was walking through the front door of the trap house only to find Percy and Pre asleep. To start the day off like any other morning, Wade wanted his breakfast weed! It didn't take Wade any time to break everything up and roll up; in less than five minutes, Percy was awakened by the sweet aroma as Wade filled himself with his early morning breakfast.

Yep! just like Wade thought. Percy was up like clockwork walking towards him.

"Pass dat shit cuz." Percy said reaching out his right hand while using the other to wipe the cold from his eyes.

"Naw nigga go brush yo shit!" Wade said, looking dead serious.

"Nigga I don't be complaining when you ask to hit my shit," Percy said as he grabbed the blunt outta Wade's hand.

"That's because I brush my shit!" Wade firmly stated.

"Fuck you nigga," Percy quickly responded.

"Naw fuck you with yo nasty ass," Wade replied.

Just as Percy and Wade were going through the motion, a knock came from the front door. Wade jumped up from the couch and grabbed the A.K. 47 before walking to the window and peeking out of it.

"Nigga put dat shit down ain't nobody at da door, but a bitch," Percy said, looking at the camera. "Bruh, move and put da stick away."

Percy walked over to the front door and opened it.

"Hey! Ummm….is Pre here?" the girl asked.

"Who you?" Percy said, looking her up and down… baby was kind of sexy, and she was a redbone.

"Tasha! Damn nigga. Now is Pre here?" Baby was getting vexed, but Percy ain't see that shit.

"Hold up," Percy said as he slammed the door in her face. Seconds later, Pre came to the door and opened it.

"Hey girl, come in," Pre said, stepping to the side to let her in. Percy and Wade were sitting on the couch smoking, looking at her, like who you is. When Pre closed and locked the door, she introduced Tasha.

"Percy, this is my best friend, Tasha, and Tasha dis is my baby Percy." Then Pre looked over at Wade.

"And Wade...dis is Tasha," Pre said in a sarcastic manner.

Tasha came over and took a seat next to Wade, letting it be known he was checking her out. Off the top, Tasha was feeling Wade in the worst way, and just off his appearance, Tasha knew he was getting major dough. Everything on him was brand new, from the hat on his head down to the shoes on his feet.

Wade and Tasha vibed a little bit, while getting to know each other better. The whole time they were kicking it, Percy had the blunts in the rotation coming back-to-back. Percy smoked so much that he became hungry, and his stomach was touching his back.

"Ay man...I don't know about y'all, but I'm starving; y'all wanna get sum' thin to eat?" Percy asked as he got up and walked into his bedroom, leaving the three alone, so he could get dressed. Pre, Tasha, and Wade continued to vibe. A couple of minutes later, Percy exited the room clean like a whistle from head to toe and walked back into the front room only to find the three still smoking.

"Come on y'all let's go," Percy said, grabbing his car keys and pistol from the kitchen table.

Friday Night...9:37 pm
Chapter 7

K-Dog and Lil Coon had just arrived at Pac man spot down in North Miami...Homestead. Today was the day for Pac Man to put his money where his mouth was...$40,000 was placed on his best dog.

K-Dog knew Money Boy was gonna handle his business; Money Boy's bloodline was bred deep, and it was one of a kind, making him a special, rare dog. Money Boy's parents were Grand Champion undefeated.

Upon arriving at Pac Man's spot, K-Dog exited the vehicle and walked towards the crowd to do some side betting while Lil Coon took care of Money Boy. Minutes later, after K-Dog made his bets, everybody walked inside the backyard, which of course, was a secluded place. Lil Coon had entered the pit with Money Boy, placing him between his legs and getting him ready to get down to business.

"You'll ready, homie?" K-Dog asked.

"Hold up, Lil Coon, he is coming now," Pac man said, looking over his shoulder at his handler as he was bringing his best dog to the dog pit. Seconds later, when the handler finally entered the pit with Pac Man's dog, they both faced the dogs off, preparing them to fight... you know, getting them to hype up for the first scratch.

"You ready," Pac Man questioned him.

"Yeah, man," Lil Coon responded

"Ok...on da count of three release em'"...1...2...3." They both let their dogs go. Both dogs charged at each other hard, and when they collided, the impact was so powerful that it made the crowd of people go crazy.

Money Boy went for the other dog's mouth, grabbing it and locking down on it. The other dog was tryna break loose, doing every trick in the book, but Money Boy wasn't having that. He was biting hard and shaking the other dog down like a rag doll.

"That's right; Money Boy get dat money, K-Dog yelled out loud.   "Some kind of way Pac-Man's dog was able to break Money Boy's lock, by peeling him off his mouth, while at the same time going for Money Boy's front leg. That was the wrong mistake because Money Boy went right back into the dog. While ripping tissues his apart, blood immediately started gushing.

For fifteen minutes straight, Money Boy stayed locked in the same spot, applying pressure, but the other dog wasn't laying either.

"Let me get a scratch, bruh," the dude said while grabbing his break stick.

Lil Coon grabbed his break stick as well, inserting it into Money Boy's mouth and breaking his lock. Why did he do that? Money Boy started acting like a fool, hollering like he had lost his damn mind.

Lil Coon turned Money Boy around, f away from the other dog, while the dude did the same. After the thirty count, they both faced the dogs off, releasing them on the three count.

Both dogs collided again on the second scratch, but this time Pac-Man's dog grabbed Money Boy by the neck and slammed him to the ground.

"Oooh!" the crowd went wild because this was the first time the other dog was able to do his thing, but only for a few seconds.

"Tighten up, boy, and get him up off ya! K-Dog yelled while clapping his hands.

Since dogs were pure-gamed A.P.T (American Pitbull Terries), they could peel each other off one another, breaking locks using tactics. Both dogs were busted up really bad and blood was everywhere, but that didn't stop them from trying to tear each other into pieces.

The fight lasted for two hours straight until both dogs were at their peak; Money Boy and Pac-Man's dog were both locked, not doing anything.

"Break em up...da scratch is now on you, Lil Coon," Pac-Man said, hoping Money Boy wouldn't cross the scratching line.

After breaking the dogs up, both sides knew that their dogs were fatigued, but this is what they look for in the dog game. Which one last longer than the other?

Once the thirty seconds were over, they released their dogs. Money Boy charged and went for the other dog's mouth, which was his favorite spot. Money Boy Grabbed the other dog's mouth biting down hard, so hard it made the other holla. Teeth and bones were all you could hear being crunched as the dogs fought for over two hours, but now it was Money Boy who was on top.   After another thirty minutes or so, they broke the dogs up and started the thirty second count; it was Pac-Man's side to get a scratch. They faced their dogs off and started the three count. Pac-Man knew his dog wasn't gonna make it on the release; he ran over and picked his dog up. That's all Pac-Man wanted to see was his dog cross the line; that was good enough for him. Live to fight another day was the only thing going through his head.

***

Lil Javon joined a gym where he learned to box. Monday through Friday, 4:00 pm to 8:00 pm, is where he spent most of his time training. Bangs Boxing Gym had top notch fighters of all ages, beginning at   six-years-old, and   all fighters were good.

K-Dog was standing along the ringside, telling Lil Javon to stick and move as he sparred with a kid who had already won fifteen amateur fights in a row. K-Dog had to admit to himself that Lil Javon was doing good after signing him up four months ago. Maybe, just maybe, if he sticks with it, Lil Javon might have a good chance to become a professional.

Watching Lil Javon closely, K-Dog observed how he threw each punch correctly, and how his movements were swift like Mayweather. The buzzer went off, signaling both fighters to stop and return to their corners.

"How you feelin champ?" K-Dog asked as soon as Lil Javon sat down. Round one was over, and it was almost time for the second round.

"I feel gud, dad," Lil Javon energetically responded.

"Aight, then listen...see you gotta stick and move...jab jab...one-two...move from side to side... punch and move," K-Dog was showing him what he wanted him to do. "When he throws his left hand, slide to da side and hit him, one to the body, one to the head," K-Dog instructed.

"Aight, dad, I got dis," Lil Javon said, smiling to himself as he stood up to get ready for Round 2. The buzzer went off, and just like that, both fighters were in front of one another, throwing punches. Some were connecting while the others hit nothing but air. Lil Javon was outboxing the kid and decided to play around with him by dropping his hands, and when he did, the kid hit with a good punch shaking him up a little.

Bing! The bell rang. As soon Lil Javon walked over to the corner, K-Dog was waiting. I told you to stick and son, he's bigger than you. Use yo jab like you been doing and stop playing...wat you playing fo? All Lil Javon could do was shake his head because he knew better.

"Now get back out there and finish him," K-Dog demanded.

***

2:15 PM

K-Dog was in route to see the girl from the strip club, the one Lil Coon introduced to Cinnamon. Twenty minutes later, K-Dog was pulling up to a nice townhouse out in Western, not too far from the Saw Grass Mall.

Cinnamon got a Lil class about herself, K-Dog thought to himself as he exited his vehicle. K-Dog walked towards the front door and knocked; seconds later, the front door to the townhouse opened; standing before him was Cinnamon looking good enough to eat. When entering her house, everything was white, from the carpet to the furniture, even the clothes Cinnamon had on was white.

K-Dog was surprised as he examined her layout, but

what caught his eyes was that fat thang sitting between her legs, looking like a camel toe.

"Hola Papi," Cinnamon said, walking up to K-Dog and kissing him on his lips.

"Hey, sexy, you miss she asked.

"Si Papi," Cinnamon responded.

K-Dog liked Cinnamon as a friend, but it was only one thing that he had to get used to, not having a conversation. This was K-Dog's fourth time coming over to Cinnamon's place, and each time was like the first: mind-blowing. And besides, Cinnamon had the meanest fuck game out this world; Pinky or none o the porno star had shit on her, let alone touch her.

K-Dog was sitting in Cinnamon's living room smoking a fat ass blunt when all of Cinnamon suddenly walked in front of K-Dog and started taking all her clothes off while simultaneously talking that Spanish shit, which of course, K-Dog couldn't comprehend.

Cinnamon pointed towards K-Dog's dick, indicating what she wanted; k-Dog wasted no time as he pulled out his dick in a flash and continued smoking. Cinnamon got down on both knees and crawled until she was between his legs. Just the sight alone made K-Dog horny; his dick was standing like the Statue of Liberty... at attention.

Cinnamon politely grabbed his dick and started licking the tip of it like a lollipop as she stared into K-Dog's eyes before going down on him, letting the warmness of her mouth cover him as she deep throated him. Ten minutes later, he was busting all in Cinnamon with only one thing on his mind... penetrating.

Green Light...Lil Coon
Chapter 8

Even though Killa was out of the game, he still had to walk lightly after being informed by a police officer on his payroll that Detective Graham was seeking revenge for the death of White Boy Bruce. To get Detective Grahams off his back Killa will have to get him dealt with because once Detective Grahams get on your trail... you might as well say your ass belongs to him.

Killa decided to meet up with Lil Coon, who was happy to put Detective Graham out of his misery. Once he received the green light, it would be time for Lil Coon to put this cracker to rest. He couldn't wait to put a bullet in Detective Graham's head.

Lil Coon was sitting outside of a bar watching Detective Grahams waiting for a perfect time to strike; he sat ten minutes before exiting his vehicle. He walked right into the bar, which of course was packed with customers, just as cool as an expert killer, and sat at the bar before placing his order.

Once receiving his drink, he looked around, sipping his Hennessy, keeping a close eye on Detective Grahams as he talked with a lady friend. Graham(s) didn't know that death was only a few steps away because he was too busy getting drunk even to recognize the signs of the destruction of death.

The drinks Detective Grahams was throwing back made him excuse himself from the table, leaving the nice-looking pale skin by herself. Lil Coon waited until he entered the restroom before getting up and walking in. Look to his surprise, When Lil Coon walks into the restroom, he sees Detective Grahams relieving himself. Lil Coon walk up behind him, drawing his murder weapon, and placed the gun barrel to the back of Detective Graham's head, which had a four-inch silencer. Lil Coon pulled the trigger without words spoken, and splattered his brains all over the restroom walls.

Mission Complete.

***

Club Dungeon was so packed with niggas and hood bitches that it didn't make any sense. Today was amateur night for strippers trying to make a name for themselves.

Bitches from Sun Land, known as "The City", was posted up, looking to stomp a mud hole in anybody's ass... Niggas too. To make matters worse, you also had niggas outta Sun land posted up smoking dirties (weed mixed with coke). These are some cutthroat niggas, so seeing them in the building tonight only meant one thing...you had to stay on point.

Shavon was at the bar serving drinks looking good as ever, and the money flow of the liquor was coming by the hundreds, not to mention, the night was still early. At the same time, Shavon was serving drinks when some dude walked up with a mouth full of gold teeth and dreads.

"Ay, Lil mama, check it out right quick, sexy" the dude

said as Shavon walked up to where he was.

"Hey, how can I assist you?"

"I was wondering if I can buy you a drink or bottle; just let me know," he said, smiling, showing all thirty-two golds. Shavon just looked at him like he was crazy. "Naw, I'm gud...but thanks for asking," she dryly responded.

"Well, at least take my number down and give me a call after the club," dude said, as he wasn't trying to let Shavon slip through the cracks that easily.

Shavon kind of got irritated. "Look! okay... I got people; he's the owner of this establishment," she said, hoping he would pick up on what she was telling him before walking off to take another customer's order leaving the dude thirsty.

"Hey, gurl!" Peachez said, walking up to the bar butt-ass naked, "Let me get a Long Island Tea."

"I got ya boo" seconds later, Shavon returned her drink.

"Here you go, boo" she said.

"Thank you," Peachez said, taking a sip from her cup. "Dis shit too live tonight."

"Hell yeah!" Shavon looked around for the first time.

"Imma be right back. I gotta get dis money dez niggaz throwing" Peachez walked off, grabbing money as it fell from the sky.

The Y.G.s had it going on in their section; money was flying like they had a money machine. Strippers were trying to get in where they fit in... but to rock with these niggas you had to be a bad bitch.

Ass and titties were everywhere, bitches were butt-naked standing on top of tables dancing in a group. Coco and China were dancing before the Y.G.s who made it a thunderstorm.

The show Coco and China were putting on had turned

into a porno show; these bitches were eating each other pussies in a 69 position. Everybody stopped what they were doing to watch Coco and China. It was supposed to be an amateur night for the young up-and-coming bad strippers, but tonight these two bitches stole the show.

After the club, the Y.G.s had to grab China and Coco's fine asses before leaving. Everybody was walking out of the club, heading to their vehicles. Shidd... you even had niggas posted up standing next to their tricked-out vehicles trying to catch someone.

Everything was going well until the same dude who tried to holla at Shavon walked up to a bunch of young crazy niggas with that drunk shit. This nigga had to be death struck or be on some kind of drug.

"Ya'll think ya'll got shit on lockdown because ya'll check boyz?" These young niggas had choppers on deck and were inching to flip any nigga.

"Wuz up with fooly," one of the Y.Gs said, grabbing the stick from the trunk, cocking it, and putting one in the head.

"Nigga get da fuck on before I flip yo ass," the young nigga said, walking up to buddy.

"I ain't gonna do shit...fuck ya'll!" That's all it took. The young nigga upped his stick and hit him dead in the gut, flipping him right out of his shoes: man down...another nigga got flipped for being dumb.

Words of Wisdom
Chapter 9
Percy

Percy was sitting at the table counting money when a knock came at the door. He quickly grabbed the remote control and pressed the mute button. To Percy' surprise, it just his cousin Shavon, so Percy got up and opened the door.

"Hey, cuz!" Shavon said while giving Percy a big hug.

"Wuz up, big head," he responded before stepping to the side and letting her in.

"Where is Lil Coon at?" she asked.

"At the crib as usual. Oh! by the way, cuz, do you know who got shot at the club a couple of weeks ago in the parking lot?"

"Nah, cuzzo, I had heard bout that shit, though; they said buddy was on some real superman type shit."

"I don't know cuz, dude probably was on them pills or sumthin," Shavon said while she walked to the kitchen and opened the refrigerator door. "What the fuck?" P, why did you get all these damn bricks just sitting here in the open like this?

"They were waiting to be sold," Percy responded.

All Shavon could do was shake her head as she grabbed the jug of juice.

"Where Wade at? she asked.

"Oh, you know he's in the back room. He is probably laying down or sumthin'.

Shavon yelled out for Wade; he ended up coming out of the room with a choppa in his hand.

"Ohhhh!! What they do, fam?" Wade said, walking excitedly into the front room to greet her.

Shavon already knew her cousins were crazy but seeing it firsthand was another story. She asked, "This what y'all do all day, sell dope and smoke weed? Ain't no telling what the hell else y'all got going on."

"Cuz, trapping is a way of life. It ain't just some hobby or sumin to do," said Percy, who was lighting up a blunt.

"Boy, I know that, but ain't you gonna at least invest some of the money into a legitimate business and clean up da money you were makin?" She couldn't help asking.

"I'm workin on openin a motor and a paint shop, but I'm 50 grand short," Percy said, sounding like Trick Daddy.

"Yea cuz, we tryna put somethin together, you know, do it real big," Wade said, hoping Shavon would leave the subject alone.

"I hope so because dis shit doesn't last forever!" was all Shavon said.

The three of them chilled out for hours at the trap house; Shavon had to admit that they were making boo coo money in dis two bedroom apartment.

Customers were coming non-stop, spending big bucks; Shavon watched Percy make $15,000 in less than two hours.

Percy wanted to get a bottle so he could get his drink on; some grabbed some money along with his fi.

"Ay y'all let's go to J & L's; I wanna get a bottle of Remey" Without being asked, the three of them exited the trap and got inside Shavon's Benz S.U.V.

Twenty minutes later, they were pulling up to J & L's parking lot; Percy got out and entered the liquor store. Wade had to piss real bad, so he got out to relieve himself.

Out of the blue, while Wade was pissing, an all-white A8 Audi, pulled up, and three dudes hopped out and approached Wade; of course, he had his back turned. Shavon saw how they were acting; she knew it was on, so she hopped out, calling his name.

"Wade...Wade watch out!" She yelled. the dudes walked behind Wade and watched him, making him fall to the ground, but Wade was back before they could put the foot game on him.

"Yeah nigga you thought shit was sweet," one of the dudes said; Wade looked at him and realized it was that same nigga who he knocked out at the store. Before they could do anything, wadeWadetched out his fi and pointed it at the dude niggaz; Percy was coming out when he saw the shit goin down. Percy ran up from behind them without them noticing, grabbing his fi from his waistline cocking it, making them look back.

"Cuz wuz up?" Percy said, looking confused.

"They just walked up behind Wade, and he punched Wade, Shavon said, pointing at the dude who punched Wade. Wade

"I should bust y'all fuck ass niggaz" Wade walked up at the dude and pointed his fi dead in his face. Wade Percy wanted to shoot their asses, but Shavon stepped in after seeing what her cousin wanted to do.

"Y'all might as well go ahead and fight because we ain't finna be on no damn first 48" Shavon looked at Wade.

"Handle yo shit nigga" Wade walking up to Shavon, giving her his gun before turning around and hitting the dude in the face with a right hook and a straight left, knocking his ass out. Buddy was asleep before he hit the ground, snoring.

"Oooh shit!" Shavon said after witnessing a knockout close-up. Shavon never saw anybody get knocked out in real life, only on T.V.

"That ain't it, is it? Percy said, looking at the two dudes standing there.

"Ay man, we ain't got nothin to do with dis, was giving him a ride," one of the dudes said, copping deuces.

"Naw! y'all wasn't saying dat when y'all had me surrounded, "Wade said, walking up in buddy's face, who was talking and knocked him out. Wade turned towards the last one left; just as Wade was about to hit him, he took off running.

"Scary ass nigga!" Percy yelled out.

"Come on before po-po pull up," Shavon said, walking towards the vehicle.

***

Later that night...

Percy had left Wade at the trap while he went to holla at K-Dog, who wanted to speak with him. When Percy Pulled up in the K-Dog's driveway, he parked and got out. Percy walked towards the front door and knocked; within seconds, the door opened, and Dominique was standing there looking like a Goddess.

"Hey, Percy, how are you? Dominique said, smiling.

"I'm good, Ms. Williams," he responded.

"Come on in, honey" Dominique stepped to the side,

letting him in.

"Kenny, baby...Percy is here!" she hollered.

"I'm in my office, boo...send him to me!" K-Dog yelled back.

"Follow me" Dominique led Percy down a hall that was soo long; it was like she was taking him on a tour. When they reached the end of the hall, there were two large double doors. Dominique pushed both doors, letting Percy in, before closing them back... this scene looked like it came from a Mob movie.

K-Dog was sitting behind his desk smoking a Cuban Cigar, looking like the boss he was.

"Have a seat, son," K-Dog said.

Percy greeted him before sitting down. .

"Wuz good witcha K-Dog?" Percy asked as he took his seat.

"You know me, my man, living... tryna stay above water." K-Dog responded.

"I feel you on dat big dawg."

"So, how is business going for ya?" K-Dog said, getting right down to business.

"Er'thang been going good Boss; I been making soo much money since you put me on, I don't know what to do... but to thank you".

"No problem, but see when you dealin with dis game, it's rules and levels to dis shit Lil One...feel me? "K-Dog explained as he took a pull from his Cigar, letting smoke come from his nose and mouth at the same time, before speaking again.

"Money is the root of all evil...money can change you, and money can make you lose focus on what's important if you ain't careful. One thing about dis game, is it doesn't last forever; that's why you get in while it's gud". K-Dog paused for a second before he continued. "One moment you got it, and just like dis... in a snap of a finger, it's gone."

Percy was paying extra close attention to what the fuck K-Dog was saying.

"It's good to see you are making a name for yourself, but at the same time, what you are going to do if the (Pigs) come kickin yo shit it with everything you got inside, God forbid? Dis why you get in and make yo money and invest it before it's too late. You have made enough money to open a business or two," K-Dog stopped talking to make sure he had Percy's attention.

"Listen, young blood Imma be the first to tell you ain't no future in distributing drugs forever. Da dope game is a steppingstone, and if you decide to make a career outta it... it's only gonna end two ways... life in Fedz or in early grave."

The two of them were talking for hours; K-Dog was breaking a lot of shit down to him about the rules of the game before ending their conversation. While K-Dog was walking Percy towards the front door, Diamond ran out of nowhere yelling... Percy Percy Percy!!!"

Family outing...K-Dog
Chapter 10

Only the strong survive mentally in this cruel, cold world; you gotta always be on point by staying three to four steps ahead. And that's what K- Dog did; regardless of what obstacles came his way, he stuck to the stripe. Not too many niggaz make it out the ghetto from selling drugs to being a powerful, rich, successful nigga all over the state of Florida to the U.N. Now that's what you call being bossed up. Dominique was the one who helped brighten K-Dog's vision, so he could see and look at the future more clearly. Everything about Dominique was different; from the moment K-Dog laid eyes on her, he knew she was special; K-Dog had to make Dominique his. Not only did K-Dog make it out, but he brought everybody who was a member of the Take Over team along with him. He even gave back to his community, which was a big thing in his book because K-Dog knew what it felt like to live in poverty. Never forget where you come from, or you'll never reach where you tryna go.

K-Dand Dominique decided to take Javon and Diamond to Walt Disney World for a family outing. Diamond was so excited that she stayed awake the whole 2 1/2 hours' drive talking about Minny and Mickey Mouse. Lil Javon played his hand Play Station. while Diamond went on and on about

Disney World

"You reached your destination, less than a quarter of a mile turn left," the G.P.S system said. Moments later, K-Dog was pulling into Walt Disney World. "We here, daddy, we here!" Diamond was jumping up and down in her seat." Jay, we here, big brotha!'

"Yep, we here," Javon said, looking around.

Once exiting their vehicle, they all went in... to check-in with luggage in hand. After paying for their room, they all got on the elevator and went to their suite. Twenty minutes later, they were back out hand-in-hand, excited to explore Walt Disney World.

The four of them got on ride after ride and even took pictures with all the cartoon characters. Cotton candy, candy apples, and had the Diamond feeling like a true Princess; nothing mattered to her. . It was all about her. And K-Dog went out his way, making damn sure his little Princess wanted for nothing.

Two whole days were a journey for Diamond; she went down the yellow brick road with Alice and the rest of the cartoon characters. K-Dog loved every minute of it, just seeing Diamond and Javon's faces light up had him feeling good.

Monday morning, the crew was back on the road heading back Down South...I-95 South Bound, but Diamond didn't wanna leave to her. It was a dream come true; she cried and cried until her little eyes couldn't take it anymore, and just like that, she was out like a light bulb.

Around 2:00 pm, there were pulling up in the driveway; Diamond was still sleeping when they pulled up. She stayed awake excited the whole way there, but she slept the whole ride back... poor baby.

It didn't take them long to unpack when they got home; Diamond was up and running around the whole house with her Minny Mouse ears on her head. As for Javon, he was out back playing with the dog while talking on his cell phone like he had invented the English language.

While the kids played, Dominique and K-Dog hit the shower and got a quickie in , which seemed like an hour. Around 6:45 pm, dinner was cooked and served; after the four of them ate, they all gathered in the living room to watch a movie.

***

11:35 pm

Members of the Y.G's were throwing a birthday/block party for one of their members, named Turk. Turk was the only young nigga outta the Y.G.'s riding around in a platinum orange Benz truck, sitting on 32's.

Turk was a check boy who was well-known Florida; all the bitches had a thang or two for him, not because he was young and getting boo-coo money, but because everywhere he went, he showed love. Turk was the type of nigga who would look out for you if you needed something. , Alot of niggas held hatred in their hearts torward Turk, simply because he was on the come up.

K-Dog and Killa had to show their faces at the Turk's party. This was the talk of the year, and besides, everybody was there showing love, but Percy killed the show when he pulled up in a brand-new Bugatti. This nigga's shit was sticking out like a unicorn in traffic, and bitches pussies started to get wet just off the sight alone.

The party was jam-packed, and it was hard for anyone to breathe. Then there were vehicles sitting on big boy's tires, from American old school to imports. Niggaz were posted up next to their vehicle's shooting ceelo (dice) on the side of the roads, bitches were everywhere walking around designer-down hoping to run across a nigga who's trying to spend some bandz.

While the block party was going on, Turk's brother, Greedy, came through on his 250 Rx dirt bike, on one wheel acting a fool. Shit was a way too live for anybody to miss out, so they knew it was the place to be. Inside of the main house where Turk had the deejay doing his thang, it was also packed and strippers were walking around butt ass naked dancing for all the big timers.

Lil Coon was posted up with the rest of them niggaz shooting dice and talking cash shit, as usual, straight putting on. Standing off to the side from where Lil Coon was shooting dice, Turk was hollering at this bad bitch named, Keisha.

Keisha was light brown, standing 5'7, weighing 140 lbs; her body was built like a stripper...Perfect...Flawless! Everything about Keisha, from her clothes to jewels, was top of the line; her vehicles were foreign, and this bitch was from Orlando. Free band gang was the only lifestyle Keisha was accustomed to.

Turk's baby mama walked up to him while he was vibin with Keisha and hit her dead in her shit, knocking her to the ground and started kicking her like she was a rag doll. This party was so straight off the chain that it didn't make any sense, and to make it more live, the Ft. Lauderdale police department never came thru or nothin; thanks to K-Dog and Killa, they were the main reason why the party wasn't closed. They had officers on their payroll, plain and simple. Around

6:15 A.M., the sun started to rise, which meant one thing, grab a group of bitches, and hit the motel. But for K-Dog and Killa, that was out of the question because they had a family to go home to, let alone have a dime piece laying in the bed naked.

Blinded by Money
Chapter 11
Percy

Percy was at Jay Dubb's car wash getting his new Bugatti fully detailed while hollering at a few bitches. Wade was sitting in Percy's Bugatti getting his dick sucked while at the same time talking on his cell to another bitch.

An hour later, Percy was pulling out into traffic clean as a whistle, heading to Sunland...The City. Bitches were trying to pull Percy and Wade over on every corner; there were even bad bitches jumping in their vehicles trying to get some play... we call those types...Rim Chasers... ain't get for nothing but a quick fuck.

This Lil freak, Indian was riding behind Percy, trying to get him to stop; this lil bitch was a straight jump-off action. Once Percy realized who was riding behind him, he automatically pulled over, letting the driver's window as she was walking up.

"Boy, when you gonna stop playing with a bitch and go head and beat dis pussy? "Indian said, leaning into the window, sticking her ass out for people to see in traffic as they passed by.

Percy has been trying to catch this lil bitch for a minute, but she wasn't fucking with him because of Pre.

"You be the one playing... shiddd." Percy reached out, slapping her dead on the fat part of her ass.

"Oooh, daddy, I like dat" Indian said, shaking her ass cheeks.

"I tell you what, lil mama, meet me at Plantation Inn, off Broward and 441," Percy got right to point.

"Boy where yo gurl at and wuz her name...Umm... Pre!" she said.

"Man, listen fuck all dat, you gonna meet me at da room or what?"

She thought about it for a minute or two. "I'd follow behind you," she walked off and got in her vehicle.

15 minutes later, Percy was pulling up in Plantation Inn's parking lot, parking in front. Percy got out and paid for the room. Moments later, the three of them were entering the room one at a time and before the room door closed good enough, Indian came out of all her clothes. Percy had to admit to himself , Indian still had the finest lil body he had ever seen thus far. He had to take pictures of her and video her as they both took turns fucking the air out of her.

***

Since Percy copped the top of his new Bugatti, niggaz have been tryna catch him slipping. The other day, Percy had a shootout with some niggaz in broad daylight. Not only was he attracting Jack Boyz, but Percy was also attracting the Alphabet Boyz too. This is the type of shit Percy lived for, so to him, his situation was give or take.

Percy was still trapping making money overlooking the fact that he was the center of attention... meaning a big ass target. But how could you tell a nigga to do anything when he never had shit?

After taking K-Dog's advice, Percy decided to put some young niggaz in the trap and let Wade run it while he fell back and invested in a legit business, a laundry mat, hoping this would keep the Feds from running down on him.

Within six months after opening the laundry mat, the Feds kicked in the house door he bought in Palm Beach. Days later, after kicking in Percy's door, the Feds also ran down on the Jitts who was trappin in his dope shot and kicked the door down as well... Wade happened to be the only one who was still running around after the Feds apprehended Percy and his workers.

***

4 months later...

Percy was sitting in the holding cell in Broward County Main Jail, waiting to see if the judge would grant him his motion. Percy's attorney had filed a motion on his behalf concerning posting a bond.

The Feds had Percy on conspiracy charges, which was mandatory life if convicted. All the inmates praised Percy like he was Scarface; even the deputies who worked at the jail were treating him differently from the rest of the inmates.

While Percy was sitting in the holding cell politicking amongst the other inmates waiting to go to court, his name was called.

" Percy Howard!"

"Right here," Percy said, standing up.

"Please step out of the cell," the deputy said, giving him an order. Percy followed the deputy's instructions and did what he was instructed to do.

After being shackled and chained, the deputy escorted Percy to the elevator.

"Dine" the elevator doors open, and Percy and the deputy step off.

The deputy led Percy down a long ass hall before approaching a set of large doors, walking him right into the courtroom.

Pre, along with Shavon, was sitting inside the courtroom when Percy entered; there were other people in there as well who were waiting for the judge to arrive. Within ten minutes, the courtroom started to get full by seconds.

Percy knew the Feds really didn't have shit on him. . The only thing the Feds had on him was the new Bugatti; they knew Percy was a member of The Take Over family and sold drugs, which Percy did for a living. But that still wasn't enough evidence to indict Percy, and they knew it, too, but that didn't stop them from locking him up, hoping to get one of his workers to roll on him.

Feelings Resurfacing
Chapter 12
Lil Coon

Lil Coon and Myesha were no longer fucking around; Myesha got fed up with Lil Coon and decided to break it off with him. Lil Coon hadn't heard from Myesha since he started fucking around with Shavon.

Lil Coon was sliding through the City in his 73 droptop donk sitting on the 30s when his cell started going off.

"Hello," Lil Coon answered it while blowing the horn as he passed by a group of chicks.

"Long time no hear from," the other person said.

"Who dis is?"

"Boy dis Myesha."

Lil Coon got silent for a while; just hearing the name and her voice had him feeling some way.

"Hello...you still there?"

"Yeah, I'm here," Lil Coon snapped back to reality.

"Oh, okay... well, I was just calling you to see how you were doing, and besides, I haven't heard from you in a while."

The truth is, Myesha was having problems with the new

dude she was seeing and needed a friend to comfort her. And the only person who came to her mind was Lil Coon.

"I been doing good you know tryna get dis money, but ummm... wuz been going on with you?" just by Myesha's hesitation, he automatically knew something was wrong.

"L...L been hangin in there tryna..."

"Myesha wuz up, wuz wrong?" Lil Coon asked, cutting her off in a mid-sentence.

"And what makes you think something wrong?"

"Listen, Myesha, I know you better than you think. I do, and I know when somethingis wrong with you," Lil Coon sympathized.

"Boy ain't nothing wrong with me," she said, putting her guards up. ...Damn...How could I be crazy enough to call Lil Coon knowing he would pick up on my voice when something was wrong? she thought to herself.

"Aight, my bad, anyway, where you at... Miami?" he inquired.

"Well...if you ask me, do I live in Miami? Yes, but I'm not in Miami at this very moment."

"Ok, dats wuz up...where are you at dis moment?"

"I'm in Lauderdale this very moment," she shot back.

"Well, I'm finna slide up on you right quick; where you at?" Lil Coon was not trying to lose the only chance to see her.

But deep down inside, Myesha wanted to see him just as badly as he wanted to see her.

"I tell you what, can you meet me on Broward at the Wings and Thangs restaurant?"

"I'd be there in ten minutes." Lil Coon ended the call and put the pedal to the metal, bringing the 454 big block motor to life.

In less than ten minutes, Lil Coon was pulling into the parking lot in his candy paint, blue Donk and jumped out.

Myesha was still sitting in her vehicle when Lil Coon pulled up looking like Money Mayweather... Damn! She said to herself as she exited her B.M.W. 328i coup.

Lil Coon was sporting an iced-out diamond crushed necklace; ; even the gold Rolex he wore had diamonds too.

"Hey, sexy," Lil Coon said, walking up to Myesha, hugging her as he politely slapped her ass.

"Look at you boy, looking like you hit the power ball or something" Myesha stepped back, admiring how fine Lil Coon was looking; he even put on a few extra pounds.

"Shidd... you ain't lookin to bad yo self."

"Boy, stop it," Myesha said, blushing from ear to ear. Lil Coon knew she was lusting over him because it was written all over her face. Seeing Myesha and how she was all dolled up, especially that fat ass of hers, had him thinking about one thing... sex.

The two talked for a while, getting updates about each other lives, but the whole time they were talking, Myesha's panties started getting wet, which meant only one thing... she wanted to fuck Lil Coon brains out. Myesha was hoping to luck up and get some dick before returning to Miami. But these memories kept playing in her head over and over again, on how Lil Coon used to fuck her and at the same time make love to her, giving her the satisfaction that her body deserved.

Emotions were running hot and deep between the two as they both stood inches away. What the hell with this? Lil Coon thought to himself. It's either now or later fuck it; he went in for the kill.

"If you thinking da same thing I'm thinking, then follow me."

"Okay!" she blurted, catching him by surprise.

"Aight," Lil Coon leaned forward and gave Myesha a big wet ass kiss before he turned around. Myesha was staring him down as he walked back to his Donk.

"I'm fuck this nigga brains out," she said to herself.

***

Shortly after pulling up to Holiday Inn, Myesha sat inside her vehicle as Lil Coon went and paid for the room. Ten minutes later, Lil Coon opened the room door stepping to the side for my Myesha to enter.

The first thing Lil Coon did after locking the door was search the room, making sure everything was straight.

Myesha sat on the edge of the king-size bed and watched Lil Coon as he rolled up some purp; she was totally in her feelings about him because this was the same nigga that she was once in love with. All the feelings she thought were gone had now come running back to her at once.

As for Lil Coon being that nigga, his reputation speaks for itself: Money…Murder…Sex.

Even though Lil Coon was fucking with Shavon, Myesha would always have a special spot in his heart, and that's something only a few can say.

Lil Coon, feeling of the effect of the hydro, got up and stood in front of Myesha and started kissing her passionately. Myesha was hotter by the seconds as she returned the kisses.

Juices started running between Myesha's inner thighs, wetting the insides of her panties. Lil Coon couldn't wait to fuck her; his dick was on brick…"fuck this shit," Lil Coon said to himself.

Next, he lustily tell Myesha, "Take these clothes off," and just like that, she started to strip until they were both butt naked before climbing into the bed. Myesha laid down on her back and spread her legs; she used her index finger, inserted it into her pussy, and started fingering herself, pussy juices were running down her fingers as she played with herself.

Lil Coon couldn't take it anymore, so he climbed between her legs and dived in face first... Splash!!

Baby girl
Chapter 13
Killa

Ever since Detective Grahams was put to rest along with his nephew White Boy Bruce, Killa didn't have to worry about getting indicted on the charges he committed in the past... All praises go to YAHWEH.

Game Time

The Road Runners were going against Lauderdale Lakes Tigers; both were undefeated. Killer was glad to see how family, friends, and loved one's came together and support this event.

The entire park was packed with people who came to enjoy the lil league and watch two undefeated football teams go head-to-head. All the big-timers and hustlers were getting their bets on which team was going to win; big bucks were on the line as the hustlers stood on the sideline paying close attention to every play.

Big Ray, known as a big timer, was on the grill throwing down; free food from seafood to soul food was given out. You even had Max, better known as the picture man, who was also there making a killing off selling pictures.

Shavon and Dominique were serving food to the public

while Bray was sitting under the umbrella eating up a storm. Bray's stomach had gotten so huge that it was difficult for her to walk.

As for Lil Coon, he was in the parking lot with the rest of them niggaz shooting dice. Everybody was gunning for Lil Coon, hoping to break his big money ass.

For two and a half hours, both teams played their hearts out, hoping to come out on top, but only one team would win and take home a championship trophy. The Road Runners had blown the Lauderdale Lakes Tigers out, and all Killa's players had gotten broken off real good for winning the game. If you forget where you come from, you will never get to where you were trying to go.

***

Since the death of Precious, Ray'anna has been continually getting straight A's, making her an honor roll student. Killa made sure Ray'anna wanted for nothing; all Ray'anna had to do was ask, and just like that, she got it. K-Dog spoiled Ray'anna rotten to the point that she was getting her hair done twice a week. Not to mention her jewelry box was stuffed with gold necklaces, rings, and diamonds, which of course, came from China Man (The Jeweler.)

Ray'anna was already driving and wearing designer clothes; no other girl at the age of 13 had ever experienced what it felt like just for one day to the spoiled like Ray'anna... Every week, Killa allowed Ray'anna to hit the mall in whatever vehicle she chose from his collection.

1:56 am

Ray'anna exited the front door of her house with her

73

iPhone placed to hear her ear talking to her bestie. Ella and Ray'anna were doing their daily once-a-week shopping spree, where she and Ella hit the malls and spent money like it grew on trees.

Ray'anna decided to take the Range Rover because that was her favorite vehicle. Once inside, Ray'anna pressed the push start button bringing the V.12 twin turbo custom-made edition to life; she made sure her seat belt was fastened and checked everything as her father explained to her before pulling off.

Forty minutes later, Ray'anna was pulling into Sawgrass Mills' parking lot with Ella in the passenger seat. Exiting the Range Rover, they entered the large mall with one thing on their minds... spending money.

Ray'anna didn't know Ella had her boyfriend at the mall waiting with one of his friends for their arrival. Out of the blue, while Ray'anna was in the Gucci store looking for an outfit, two boys walked up and called her friend's name.

"Ella! one of the boys, called out..."Wuz gud," he said as soon Ella turned around.

"Hey, Pete!" Ella said, walking up to him and hugging him. Ella looked back at Ray'anna, hoping to have her attention, only to find Rayanna buying two Gucci outfits with a handbag to match.

Ray'anna wasn't into boys like that; she had her mind on getting an education; Ray'anna wanted to make her father proud at all costs.

Malik was Ella's boyfriend's friend who was star stuck over Ray'anna when he first laid eyes on her, he was trying to do anything to make Ray'anna notice him, but Ray'anna wasn't paying him any mind. Malik felt like he didn't exist, which caused him to feel some type of way; Malik couldn't take it any longer and decided to give Ray'anna a piece of his mind.

"Yo, Pete, wuz up with dis stuck up chick actin like she's all dat and a bag of chips" Ella and Pete looked at each other and shrugged their shoulders like, I don't know.

"Maybe she's not feeling you, bruh," Pete said.

Malik was the number one star of his basketball team at the school; all the girls at his high school were giving him all the attention. Ray'anna knew a little about boys: boys have sex with the girls, and boom, just like that, they will have a baby.

"Does she know who I am? She better ask around about me," Malik said.

Ray'anna stopped dead in her tracks as the four of them were walking. She turned about and faced Malik.

"Look, Lil boy," Ray'anna said, shaking her neck like the chicks from the projects.

"I don't give a damn who you are or what you stand for because that really doesn't mean jack to me. But one thing I'm not going to do is to let some nappy head boy disrespect me. I'm a princess." Ray'anna looked Malik straight in the eyes. "Now figure dat shit out" Rayanna gave him a hand and walked off.

Malik was cursing up a storm at Ray'anna, calling her every name in the book but the child of God.

Lil Javon and his partners were walking by and saw and heard everything. Javon and Rayanna were like family, even though Ray'anna had a crush on him. Javon waited until Ray'anna walked away before stepping in front of her.

"Ray'anna, you straight?" Javon asked, surprising the hell out of her; when she looked up and saw who it was, Ray'anna started smiling.

"Hi Javon, what are you doing out here?"

"Chillin with my homies," Javon responded, looking dead into Malik's eyes.

"Wuz up with dude, Pete, getting all in my business?" Malik asked.

Javon looked over at his friends and started laughing.

"You think shit funny or sumthin? It ain't gonna be funny if I punch you dead in yo jaw, lil nigga" Malik said, poking his chest out.

"Now hold up whatever your name is!" Ray'anna said, trying to stop the problem before it escalated.

"Dis is my people, so you could chill with all dat, cause ain't nobody on dat drama stuff."

"Naw fuck dat! If he got a problem, he can get it off his chest, "Malik said, refusing to give up.

"Listen, dude, I don't want no trouble, but I'm not finna stand here and let you disrespect her either, "Javon said, walking up in Malik's face.

"So wat you gonna do about it, lil punk-uh?" Malik pushed Javon, making him fall to the ground.

"Now you done fucked up, "Javon said, getting up from the ground. "Wuz up nigga." Javon got on his boxing stand.

"Look at dis nigga...who he thinks he is...Mike Tyson?"

Before Malik could get another word out, Javon hit him so hard on his jaw that he made Malik fall to the ground snoring...Lights out.

***

Killa was home with Bray sitting in the living room when when Ray'anna came through the door talking and bragging about how Javon knocked out ole boy for disrespecting her.

Ray'anna went on and on as Killa and Bray looked at one another; they already knew about the crush Rayanna had on Javon. Bray waited until Ray'anna ran off, talking to her friend on her cell about what took place at the mall. Bray turned to face Killa, who was shaking his head.

"Bae, what are we gonna do with her?" Bray was smiling, remembering the first time she had a crush.

"Let her be, she alright."

"Yeah, but Javon is family," Bray responded.

"They are just kids; hopefully, she will grow outta it," Killa said, smacking Bray on her butt.

"Yeah, okay, let her grow outta it my butt; when we were her age, don't act like you wasn't having sex. "Bray pinched Killa on the leg.

"I ain't worrying about her having sex, but I'll keep it in mind, "Killa said, confident in Ray'anna.

Pay to 2 is Boss...
Chapter 14
K-Dog

K-Dog moved Cinnamon out of her apartment into a four-bedroom house with a pool in the back. K-Dog even bought her a brand new 760 B.M.W. straight off the showroom floor. Cinnamon will never have to worry about anything for as long she's been alive; not only was Cinnamon living like a queen, but her bank account was looking like Cheerios.

Since K-Dog made Cinnamon his side chick, she decided to take English classes to speak fluently, so she could communicate a lot better with K-Dog. Cinnamon moved Season into her new house because it was too big for her to live there alone.

Season wasn't into Killa like that; yes, they hung out a few times, and they both enjoyed themselves, but it wasn't Cinnamon who was fucked up about K-Dog; Season was. . From the first time Season laid eyes on K-Dog, she wanted to fuck the brains out of him, and Cinnamon didn't mind sharing, as long as K-Dog was cool with it.

Most of the time, when K-Dog came by Cinnamon's place, Season would always let her presence be known, but K-Dog didn't know that they both were willing to share, and that's why K-Dog didn't bite the bate.

K-Dog was sitting at Cinnamon's kitchen table, eating with them. When Cinnamon stood up and walked over to where Season was sitting and sat down on her lap, Season started rubbing Cinnamon's lower back while looking into K-Dog's eyes.

"Papi, me wanna share... Si," Cinnamon said, making K-Dog stop eating as he thought to himself.

K-Dog stood up and walked in front of them, grabbing both of their hands and leading them into the Cinnamon's master bedroom.

"Take it off," K-Dog demanded as soon they stepped into the room. Both girls did not waste any time as they did what they were told; they stripped down until they were butt-ass naked.

"Papi me want to make a movie... Yes," Cinnamon wanted to record their little freak section, so she walked into her walk-in closet and grabbed a recording camera.

"Yes, Papi, we have been waiting for this moment for some time now," Season said, speaking better English.

"Take em off," Cinnamon pointed at the clothes K-Dog had on.

Season walked in front of K-Dog and started taking off his clothes while Cinnamon set up the recorder.

The three of them got into bed together, butt-ass naked; Season and Cinnamon started kissing each other as they both played with one another's pussies. K-Dog was rubbing Season's fat-shaved, pretty, pink pussy from the back, getting it wetter and wetter before inserting his fingers into Season's tight wet pussy. Damn, she tight, K-Dog thought to himself as he penetrated, fucking her with his fingers.

After seeing how wet Season was, K-Dog wanted to feel

her wetness on him. So he grabbed the base of his dick and slowly entered her, letting her walls adjust before he started beating it up.

K-Dog slow fucked Season from the back long-dicking her down, hitting rock bottom; K-dog was hitting her G-spot.

"Ooh yes, Papi, I like that," she said, arching her back.

Just the sight alone was making K-Dog feel like he was in a real ass porno movie, especially with the camera rolling; K-Dog started feeling himself.

"Switch up" K-Dog made them change positions, Season then laid down on her back, and Cinnamon had positioned herself face down, ass up.

Cinnamon had the fattest ass K-Dog seen thus far; her ass was 100 percent real. K-Dog had to bite that thang from the back before fucking her.

K-Dog couldn't fuck Cinnamon like he wanted because she was closed-built, and she couldn't take a dick.

As for Season, the baby was a straight-up dick junky; it wasn't anything for her to take the dick. She was a pro meeting K-Dog thrust for thrust, fuck for fuck.

Shit started to get wild by how K-Dog was fucking them, ass slapping, hair pulling, and a lot of choking; this was the type of shit these bitches wanted to be done to them; they were most definitely stone-cold freaks putting on for the camera.

For a whole hour straight, the three of them fucked and sucked one another dry like an empty well. Cinnamon got up with her knees wobbly and walked to where the recording camera was hooked up to the flat screen T.V., and pushed play before getting back in bed, lying next to K-Dog and Season.

Back out
Chapter 15
Percy

Percy was finally released from the County Jail after paying 10 percent of $100,000, in addition to paying restitution. The judge gave Percy a go-home pass after his attorney persuaded him by waving a bunch of crispy $100dollar bills in his face.

Percy was allowed to walk away as a free man, of course with a monitor band, and if any violations occurred, the judge would have no choice but to revoke his bond.

After Percy received his belongings from the property room, he was escorted to the house arrest office. The only good out of this is, Percy was given a black box instead of being stuck at home all fucking day.

Twenty minutes later, Percy walked back into the lobby, smiling ear to ear, when he saw Pre.

"Wuz up, baby girl" Percy walked up and gave Pre a big ass hug out this world while putting his tongue down her whole fucking throat, nasty just like she liked it.

"Damn boy, you must've missed da hell outta me" Pre stepped back, looking him up and down.

"You damn right I did," Percy responded, slapping her on her ass. "Now let's get da hell from outta dis bitch.

The Feds didn't take anything from Percy because he didn't have shit in his name; yes, he still had his hot ass Bugatti,his laundry mat, and his house as well.

The Feds weren't trying to seize any of Percy's access yet; they wanted to catch him with his hands in the cookie jar; until then, they'll lay back and keep him under heavy surveillance.

Percy knew the Feds were watching him like a hawk hoping to catch him slipping. Percy knew he couldn't get out of jail and jump back into the game headfirst. Percy had to chill and lay back because he was hot like a firecracker, so he knew what he had to do… keep his ears and eyes open.

Wade was still doing his thang, making money as he invented it while keeping a low profile.

The Feds were 38-hot when they hit the trap spot because they only confiscated 18 ounces of cocaine, twenty-six thousand in cash, two assault rifles, and three automatic handguns. The youngsters were the only individuals sitting in the trap when the Feds kicked the door down, but since they were only juveniles, the Feds couldn't do shit but give them 21 days in the Juvenile Detention Center.

The only thing going through his mind as he sat in the front room of his house was how he was gonna make money without the Feds knowing, which was impossible to figure out. Maybe Wade had some ideas because Percy needed to get his feet back wet; this was the only thought Percy had as he waited for Wade to arrive.

Ever since the Feds hit the trap and locked up Percy and his little workers, Wade started smoking like a broken-down stove, straight stressing. Then when he received a call from Percy telling him that he was out and to slide through, Wade was happy as hell listening to his cousin's voice. Hearing him talk brought a smile onto his face, something he hadn't felt in a while. Them pussy ass crackas stay tryna keep a black man down, he thought as he headed to Percy's spot.

About an hour later, after circling the block four times just to make sure Percy wasn't under the microscope, Wade pulled into the driveway and parked. He then exited his rental car locking the door behind him and entered through Percy's front door.

"Cuz, Where you at nigga?" Wade yelled.

Percy came from the back room eating a bowl of cereal, wearing a tank top, a pair of gym shorts, and NBA tube socks.

"Wuz up, my nigga!" Percy said while walking up and embracing Wade.

"Damn nigga you done picked up a few pounds," Wade said as he eyed Percy down.

"Shidd… you know how it goes up in dat bitch, da first thing a nigga does is grab the bible or work out."

"I feel you, bruh… so wuz up with the lil plan you got, cuz?" Wade said, changing the subject.

"PLAN?" Percy responded

"I thought you might have one shid… you been out here, right?" Percy said, referring to the streetz.

"Yeah, cuz"

"Aight, then what you got?"

"I got some shit I know will go good once we put it to play…now listen up nigga while I put you up on the beat," Wade said, looking straight into Percy's eyes.

Wade had a plan that would put more money in their safes; all they needed was to open another trap for six months. Wade was the one to open it up and get it jumping; then, the rest was up to the workers.

Percy had money and fifteen bricks of raw cocaine in his stash. Within thirty days, Wade got the trap jumping and handed it to his lil workers; he wanted the trap to be well-organized as possible. He had niggaz on the block watching 24/7. He even posted them with walkie-talkies, riding up and down on bikes.

Everybody had a role to play, day in and day out; no one was making more the next…$2,500 was what everyone was making weekly. Percy and Wade had the trap doing numbers; every thirty days, they were pulling in like 100k. Niggaz from all over Broward, Dade, and Palm Beach, was coming to cop that Raw…str8 clean.

Within three months, they sold thirteen bricks(Kilos) and needed to re-up; Percy had two left, so he put in his order for another fifteen bricks. Percy knew by his court date that they would sell the dope and keep it pushing.

Chapter 16
Mo money Mo murder

One Stop was the place to be on Sunday mornings. One Stop was so swoll that it was jam-packed. There were cars parked everywhere; there were even vehicles on the other side of 27th Avenue parked, straight throwing it up.

Bishop Obey Thomas drives by One Stop every Sunday for Sunday School en route to church. Every time he drives by One Stop with all that action going on, Obey Thomas is tempted. But every time, he is with his lovely wife.

Back in the 70s and 80s, Bishop was a bad boy when it came down to money. Even when it came down to shooting dice, this mufucka was a pro; he also had a special touch when he rolled them; he made them point on will.

Bishop's main thing was three-card Molly. He made a living off scheming people in all kinds of card tricks. From shooting pool to playing checkers or chess, Bishop would make bets and win 95%.

Bishop's wife was home sick with a fever and not riding with him this day as he was passing One Stop. Bad bitches were walking around with the hottest short and tightest coochies outfits. This bad redbone wore shorts that read on the back…"BOOTY." Bishop's dick started getting hard as she walked past his vehicle; the baby looked like a brick house… Megan Stallion-type shit.

"Oh my God," Bishop said out loud to himself as he grabbed his crotch area while rolling the window down. The red bone saw Bishop staring and lusting and blew him a kiss as she sucked on a lollipop.

That broke the last straw on the camel's back; Bishop couldn't take it anymore, so he busted a u-turn, ran the red light, pulled along the side of the curve with the rest of the vehicles, and got out.

Bishop was well known to everyone, so when he walked up towards Lil Coon and his crew, they all gave him daps, giving the O.G. much respect.

"Wuz gud Bishop?" Lil Coon said, giving him a firm handshake.

"I'm blessed and highly favored young man…how bout yourself?"

"I'm living in paradise," Lil Coon said, spreading his arms towards the sky.

"What brings you around my neck of the woods?"

"I just dropped by to share the word of God before I head off to church," Bishop responded, holding up his Bible while looking at all the fine women who passed by with their asses hanging out.

Lil Coon already knew why Bishop was lurking. The temptation was getting the best of Bishop, and he just couldn't resist, plain and simple.

"Kisha, y'all bring y'all asses over here and give Bishop a time of his life!" Lil Coon yelled out to a group of bad bitches. The girls walked over to Bishop and started shaking what their mama's gave them.

Bishop couldn't help himself as he watched half-naked women dance in such a way that it took him back to the days when he was living in the world. All he could do was shake his head as one of the girls walked up and started grinding on him.

"Do yo thang Bishop ...slap dat ass!" Lil Coon yelled.

Within minutes Kisha had opened Bishop up; she had him vibing. That's right, she had Bishop's nose open; as he stood behind Kisha grinding on her ass.

"Dawg dats a muthafucka hypocrite, and he is preaching the word and shit...." Sleep said to Lil Coon.

"Naw, bruh, you got it all wrong... The bible says all men are sinners and have fallen short of the glory of God," Lil Coon shot back at him, hoping he'll get the picture.

***

"Everybody knows 10th Terrace belongs to Lil Coon in the City, Not a bag of weed, let alone a nickel rock, be sold unless it comes from

Lil Coon. And if anybody tries to open up shop on his Turf, it's gone be consequences and repercussions that come behind that."

Some niggaz came out of Miami on 10th Terrace and opened up shop without doing any real study, examining, or any legal work before coming somewhere that's already taken.

A week had passed before word got back to Lil Coon or his crew. These Miami niggaz was on some kill or be killed type of shit, Zoe Pound Breed Str8 Killers.

These Haitians were heavily equipped and affiliated, so

they felt like it was enough money for everybody to eat, and if anybody had a problem, "FUCK EM."

One day while Lil Coon was handling business, he received a phone call from one of his workers who told him a bunch of Haitians outta Miami, known as Zoe Pound, had set up shop.

This was like so much music to Lil Coon's ear that it made his Trigga finger itch. It was killing Lil Coon down to his soul as he drove; he couldn't wait to put these niggaz in a coffin.

Lil Coon turned off Sistrunk onto 10th Terrace creeping real slow with Sleep in the passenger seat. Sleep bruh, you see dis shit, my nigga? Lil Coon said as they were passing by the Haitian's spot.

Yeah, homie, and look! Sleep responded, pointing to a hand-and-hand transaction goin down.

"Dez Haitians got some balls. Ah, don't worry, I got sumthin for they ass," Lil Coon said as he passed by, heading towards his trap house. Lil Coon's workers were already outside sleeping when he pulled up.

Once parked , they exited the vehicle and walked to where the workers were standing. "Wat dey do Homies? Lil Coon said as they walked up. "Same ol' shit, just another day," one of the workers said.

"Let's slide inside right quick," Lil Coon said, walking off. Tenth Terrace had a lot going on; kids were riding bikes or wheels , and even the Arab store from across the street where Lil Coon had his operation going on inside was crowded.

Niggaz were posted shooting dice next to a group of hood, project gutta bitchez, smoking weed, or just talking shit. Mom Betty was like everybody's mother in the Federals, known as the Greens.

Everybody had mad love for Mom Betty because she was the go-to person. She would have let a person stay if they needed a place to stay for a couple of days.

Just as Lil Coon was walking towards the trap spot, Mom Betty was walking outta her apartment door.

"Hey, Mom, Betty," Lil Coon said, stopping to hug her.

"Hey, sugar! How are you?"

"I'm gud Mom Betty," Lil Coon responded.

"Okay, you be careful and stay out of trouble, Ya'll hear!"

"We will, Mom Betty," Sleep said, walking up and hugging her; Sleep reached into his pockets. "Here you go, Mom Betty, go get you some cigarettes." Sleep gave her a hundred dollar bill.

"Thank you, baby! I got one more cigarette left that I been holding on for days." Ma Betty took the money and put it inside her bra.

"Now I can go to Hard Rock and try to win some Indian people money," Mom Betty said, laughing out loud.

Lil Coon and the rest of them walked into the trap before the door closed all the way... Lil Coon spoke out.

"Sleep, dez Haitians think shit is sweet dawg, setting up shop in our shit, where our bread and butter comes from!" Lil Coon sat down on the couch.

"Taking money outta our pocket. Naw, I can't have dat. Ay Sleep call up them Boyz because later tonight, I'ma bring havoc to em Haitians."

***

Later that night, around 5:00 am , Lil Coon and six other niggaz, Sleep included, had the whole house surrounded. All six of them were strapped with sticks that held 100 rounds.

Dressed in all black with ski masks on, they positioned themselves around the Haitian trap house, some in the front, some in the back, and some on the side. The whole neighborhood was peaceful and quiet; there wasn't a single soul out except for a bunch of stray dogs running around destroying people's garbage cans.

Once everybody was in position, the ones in the front started shooting the house up. The Haitians started shooting back, letting the choppas spit. The Haitians did not know that there were gunmen waiting on them. One at a time, the Haitians ran out the back door, hoping to get away, but Lil Coon and Sleep were knocking their asses down, straight flipping them out of their shoes.

In less than five minutes, Lil Coon and his crew threw them like plum juice, killing them all, before running back to their separate vehicles. Lil Coon never knew that killing these Zoe Pound niggas shit would only get worst.

Secret Weapon
K-Dog
Chapter 17

K-Dog and Killa had found out about the killing that took place days ago, and now shit had hit the fan, hard. The H.N.I.C of the Zoe Pound made contact with one of the Take Over family members and beat him half to death. They sent a message t through the member who they beat up...

Why couldn't Lil Coon just sit back, maybe for a chance, talk shit through without putting mafuckas in the dirt? Killa was thinking to himself that Lil Coon should have come forward and explained what had been going on before causing World War 3.

Killa sat across from K-Dog in K-Dog's office at the car lot, listening to a conversation between Haitian Jack and K-Dog.

"Look, Zoe, you taking it to whole notha level dat I master so well. Are you sure you really wanna take it there, behind some foot souljas that were only some pawns? And besides, that's on your end nigga" K-Dog spoke through the speaker phone.

"My end?"

"Yeah, yo end," K-Dog shot back to the Haitian, who was 38 hot...

"Shid, it wasn't Lil Coon's fault that Haitian Jack and them thought they could set up shop on the shit and not be dealt with. If he wanted to shed blood and cause mayhem behind his fuck ups, it was time to take Haitian Jack out."

"Kill the head first, and the rest of the body go follow."

The conversation between the two bosses wasn't going so great; Haitian Jack wanted war, and he made this clear before he hung up.

After K-Dog ended the call with Haitian Jack, he looked up at Killa smiling! This mothafucka got to be crazy or something... Killa thought to himself as he looked back at his right-hand man.

"Let me call my quiet assassins," K-Dog said nonchalantly as he picked up his private phone.

Friday Da 13Th, Two days later

"King of Diamonds was live like always; every bitch was in there was looking like the next Top Model. King of Diamond was only for top-notch bitchez; every dancer who danced at the King of Diamond had to be a bad bitch.

All the big ass ballers were up in the building making it snow; money was flying everywhere that it was hard to see. Money was falling out of the sky like it was snowing.

King of Diamonds was Haitian Jack's hangout spot; this is where people came to find him, but the only problem is that Haitian Jack is well-protected. Bodyguards were always smothering him heavy-armed. It wasn't easy to penetrate his security. Not only that, but Haitian Jack was fucking around in that Voodoo shit heavy.

Cinnamon and Season walked into King of Diamonds looking like Egyptian goddesses; Diamonds were all over their Egyptian clothes; every time any light landed on them as they were making their way toward the bar, the reflection of the diamonds sparkled.

By the time Cinnamon and Season reached the bar, they had everybody's attention, including Haitian Jack and his gang.

It did not take long before niggas, and gay bitches started coming out of nowhere, offering drinks or hoping to catch a bite. Cinnamon and Season rejected their asses one at a time because these bitches had a mission to complete, and by all means, they were gonna do what they came to do… EXECUTE!

The whole time Cinnamon and Season were sitting at the bar shining like the Virgin Mary, Haitian Jack had his eyes on them. He sent them both a gold bottle hoping to catch their attention, but little did Haitian Jack know he was playing right in the hands of death.

A bad stripper walked up to Cinnamon and Season butt-ass naked and offered the bottles to them as she was instructed to do.

"I think dis ladies belongs to you," the stripper said, passing them the bottles.

"Well, thank you," Cinnamon said, excepting her bottle. And who is this coming from, mama?

"Oh, the man over there," pointing towards Haitian Jack; they both looked in his direction and thanked him, and just like that, Haitian Jack invited them both over to his section.

When Cinnamon and Season walked up to Haitian Jack's

table, it looked like they were gleaming, hypnotizing Haitian Jack. Season walked up to Haitian Jack and greeted him like he was a King while Cinnamon stood on her grounds.

Haitian Jack had no idea that his hands were in Cinnamon and Season's livea as he popped bottles throwing money without a care in the world. The whole night, Haitian Jack put on Cinnamon and Season until it was time to leave.

At 5:16 am, Haitian Jack was walking out of the building tipsy. Cinnamon was under his arm while Season was under the other. The bodyguards were surrounding them as they walked with Haitian Jack, waiting for Bentley.

Once inside, Haitian Jack's chauffeur pulled off, staying in the middle of Haitian Jack's security, making it impossible for anybody to try anything.

While Haitian Jack was playing between Season's legs, Cinnamon had her tongue down Haitian Jack's throat, slowly waiting to inject their poisonous venom into his veins.

Just as Haitian Jack's chauffeur was pulling up to his mansion, Cinnamon and Season went in for the kill, slicing Haitian Jack's neck from ear to ear.

Once, the chauffeur parked and exited the vehicle having no idea what was going on and walked to the back door opening it. A bullet from a small caliber hit him between his eyes, knocking the brains out of his head.

The two exited the vehicle as if nothing happened; they both waited until their ride came before jumping in, leaving back a bunch of dead fucks, killing everything in sight.

Neva Knew
K-Dog
Chapter 18

Kill the head, and the body dies; that is what K-Dog did. He took out the King without lifting a finger, one of the laws from 48 Laws of Power, The Element of Surprise.

Capitalizing off Haitian Jack's weakness, K-Dog put two of the worst bitchez on God's green earth and used them for an easy checkmate. Zoe Pound didn't know where the hit came from; all they knew was their leader was dead.

All they knew was Haitian Jack left the strip club with two foreign bitches. Nobody knew their names or where they came from. When the police arrived at the scene, they discovered Haitian Jack, his chauffeur, and his security dead as a door knob.

The only question everybody wanted to know was, where were all the other members when all this went down? Was it a hit from the inside or what? K-Dog, along with Killa and Lil Coon was at Cinnamon's place, drinking champagne while politicking. Cinnamon and Season lay in the master bedroom facing where K-Dog was sitting with the door open smoking.

Lil Coon never knew or thought that Cinnamon and Season were cold blooded stone-cold killas.

"Dawg, I never knew they were built like that," Lil Coon said, staring at Cinnamon and Season as they lay in plain view.

"Me either," Killa said, remembering the first time he fucked Season. K-Dog had already informed Killa how trenches Cinnamon and Season were. Actually, Killa witnessed how dangerous they were when Cinnamon and Season killed a nigga in front of him.

One night in the club parking lot, some nigga tried to pull a stunt and got his neck broken. The shit happened so fast by how they both killed him. The dude pulled a pistol, and right when he pointed it, Season karate chopped the gun from his hand, then kicked him in the balls in one quick motion.

Cinnamon walked up to the dude, placing both her knees on his back while putting him in a backward headlock position. Season jumped up into the air, falling on his chest with her knees, totally breaking his neck on contact. Nobody would've thought how dangerous Cinnamon and Season really were in a million years.

"While ya'll be thinking about pleasure, nigga I be thinking about business...Ladies!" K-Dog yelled out. Cinnamon and Season got out of the king-sized bed and walked where K-Dog was sitting down by his feet like two trained dogs... Straight Submissive.

K-Dog reached down to receive the blunt; he pulled it, inhaling the smoke. "How did you ladies manage to take out Haitian Jack so smoothly?" K-Dog said, blowing the smoke out. Then, Season looked up with those lovely eyes of hers.

"Beauty, which is Power because we're able to lure our

targets in, or simply use our other weapon, 'PUSSY,' Season said, looking like an angel.

"We know all the tricks in the country; we do what we have to do, to get what mee' need Papi' and get what mee' want," Cinnamon said, caressing K-Dog's foot.

"And what's dat yall want?" Lil Coon said, looking confused!

"Papi mee' want blood," Cinnamon said, looking dead serious into Lil Coon's eyes; that shit sent chills through his body.

**

YOU KNEW WHAT YOU WERE DEALING WITH FROM DAY ONE; YEAH, I BEING YOUNG, BUT GOTTA LOTTA OLD WAYS. IT'S ONLY BEEN A FEW DAYS, SO YOU SAY YOU LOVE ME IN A MARRIED WAY....

Soulja Slim was playing in K-Dog's Range Rover as he slid through the hood. K-Dog was a made nigga, but most importantly, K-Dog never turned his back on where he came from, da hood.

Shortly after K-Dog rode through the hood, he decided to pull up on Jay Dub on 7Th andWashington Park at the studio. When K-Dog pulled up to the studio, niggaz was standing around with a bunch of bad bitchez. This wasn't anything new seeing a large group of people hanging out at Jay Dubs studio.

Once K-Dog parked, he got out wearing a Versace outfit, with the shoes to match. The crowd of people out front each embraced K-Dog, showing mad love. This nigga was a king in everybody's eyes, and that's how they treated him, like a king.

But in K-Dog's eyes, he was just a nigga who was blessed enough to make something outta nothing Taking a negative, turning it into a positive. After K-Dog greeted everyone, he walked through the front door that leads to the studio.

When K-Dog entered, Jay Dub was sitting on the couch with his feet kicked up between two bad bitchez. "What's up, my nigga?" Jay Dub said, standing up and giving K-Dog a handshake as he walked up.

"You tell me, big time," K-Dog shot back at him.

One thing about Jay Dub is this nigga is a supreme hustler; when it came down to niggaz getting money, Jay Dub's name was mentioned.

"Check me out, I got something I want you to see," Jay Dub grabbed his choppa before walking into the studio room, where the songs get recorded.

"Head, take it from the top," Jay Dub said, entering the studio. "Dis young nigga gone make me millions, watch what I say yah."

J-Head was an up and coming local rapper straight outta 954 Lauderdale. . He has been doing his thang for a while in the music industry, so he was the hottest thing in Florida. J-Head entered the booth with a bottle of V.S.O.P REMY and grabbed the headphones.

Soon as the beat took off, J-Head started spitting; K-Dog had never heard anybody spit like that before. All K-Dog could do was bop his head to the lyrics because what J-Head was spitting was that real shit.

"Diz, young nigga is the future," Jay Dub said as he looked over at K-Dog, straight zoned out.

Ten minutes later, after J-Head put the track down, he exited the booth smoking a blunt with a bottle clutched in his hand. "Dat'z dat Fi ain't it Jay Dub? J-Head said, walking up and dapping him up.

"Damn right you murdered that shit," Jay Dub responded.

"K-Dog wat dey do big homie?" J-Head said, dapping him up as well.

"I'm good, Fam a boy, you can be the next 2Pac or something," K-Dog said, admiring J-Head's talent.

"Do you think so big homie?" J-Head asked.

"Hell yeah, lil nigga," K-Dog said, looking over at Jay Dub.

"I told him the same thing," Jay Dub said. "I just can't keep him from going to jail. I just had to pay $70,000 on him to beat a murder charge,"Jay Dub shook his head, reminiscing.

I'm Back
Chapter 19
Percy

Percy was entering the courtroom with the clan. Today, the Feds had to bring everything to the table: factual information or drop all pending charges on Percy.

As soon as Percy took his seat along with the clan, his attorney approached him. "How are you feeling today, Mr. Howard?" Percy's attorney said while shaking his hand.

"I feel how I look… And I look damn good," Percy responded, adjusting his tailored suit.

"I'm just ready to walk out of this courtroom; I don't like it; it makes me feel some type of way," Percy said, shaking the jeepers off him. Listen, the Feds are gone; try to throw everything they got up their sleeves at us.

"That's why we are paying you to bat that shit down, "Killa said, cutting him off in mid-sentence.

"Mr. Howard has nothing to worry about; we'd secured him," Percy's attorney responded, smiling while walking back towards his seat.

Percy waited for an hour and a half before the judge

called him. "Percy Howard!" The judge called while looking around in the once crowded courtroom, which was now a few.

That's me, judge" Percy's attorney said as he stood up and waived for Percy to join him. Percy stood up and approached the bench alongside his attorney.

"Okay, now everybody is here; let's get down to business shall we," the judge looking at Percy's attorney. "Start with you."

"Your honor, we're here today because I filed a motion for circumstantial evidence. My client was taken into custody by the F.B.I. and charged with all kinds of charges that my client doesn't have anything to do with. Let alone know anything about it. So, I filed a motion that is in my client's best interest; the F.B.I. needs to show and have solid proof of evidence that my client commited these crimes. Or I would like for a dismissal, Your Honor," Percy's attorney argued, hitting the ball right out of the ballpark.

"Okay, State, would you like to address the courts?" The judge asked.

"Well, Your Honor, all we have are photos of the defendant taken by the F.B.I. where the drugs and firearms were located," the D.A. looked over to where the agents were signaling for help.

The D.A. knew they didn't have anything on Percy except for some pictures, which wasn't enough to convict him. So, the D.D needed the Feds to take control since they were the ones bringing the matter before the courts.

I'll let them take it over from here; the D.A stepped down, turning it over to the Feds. The Feds tried their best to convince the judge, but they didn't have facts; for that reason, all the charges brought against Percy were dropped, and he walked out of the courtroom with his head towards the sky and his chest poked out. That's right, Percy walked right out that bitch a free man.

***

Later that night, Percy and Wade hit up Club Dungeon to celebrate because Percy had beaten the Feds, and he wanted the world to know. When they arrived in Percy's Bugatti, all the attention was focused on them.

Percy pulled right up in front of the club and got out. There was no search nor hassle as they walked inside the club, hollering at a couple of hoochies before making their way towards the bar.

Shavon already had a gold bottle waiting for them; as soon as Shavon saw them approaching, she grabbed the bucket and brought it to them. "Wuz up ya'll? Shavon said as she placed the bucket down.

"We came to have a good time, "Wade responded while taking the bottle out of the bucket."

"I know that's right... Ay cuz bring me five thousand in ones, Percy said, reaching into his Robin Jeans, pulling out a Haitian knot, all one-hundred-dollar bills.

Once Shavon received the money, she went and got the ones and came back. "Here you go boy," Shavon handed the ones to Percy.

"Thanks, cuz" "Ya'll enjoy and be safe," Shavon said, walking off. Percy and Wade got up from the bar and walked in front of the stage where a dancer was hanging upside down on a pole. And they both started throwing money.

The stripper got off the pole and walked where Percy and Wade were, grabbing the cup out of Percy's hand and swallowing the whole cup of liquor in one gulp. The baby started doing her thing, shaking what her mama gave her.

And while honey put on, Percy was throwing money like crazy; Percy wanted her by any means necessary. Wade saw how Percy was acting; he immediately knew Percy was feeling her.

"Damn nigga you feelin dat bitch? "Wade asked, seeing how Percy was making eye contact.

"She's a stripper cuz" "that's it."

"Stripper my ass nigga," Wade shot back, making Percy laugh. Dat Lil bitch over there been trying to get our attention ever since we stepped in the door" Percy looked in the direction where Wade's were, only to find the stripper licking her tongue out like she was thirsty.

"Damn cuz dat bitch gotta long ass tongue," Percy said; "I know you finna see what is she talking bout, right?"

"Nigga you already know," Percy said while standing up. "I'll be right back and left."

Out of the blue, while Wade was checking his I.G., a badass stripper walked up behind him and put her hands over his eyes.

"Guess who?" the stripper said, licking his ear.

"My future wife," Wade said, grabbing her hand and pulling her around. "I see you full of surprises," Wade said making the stripper sit next to him.

"Surprise is my middle name," the stripper said, crossing her legs. Wade didn't want to waste any time other than what he had to; he got what he was looking and for now, it was time for him to bounce.

"Go get you're your shit and meet me out front."

Chapter 20
Lil Coon

One thing about niggaz outta Broward County…. Lauderdale, that is, money is always the motive. If it doesn't make dollars, it doesn't make sense. Backyard fights, shooting dice on the corner, and breaking into vehicles or houses were how they lived.

Lil Coon was pulling up at Lil Bruce's trap in Tater Town; Lil Bruce was a go-getter when it came down to money. All kind of illegal activities was going on when Lil Coon pulled up, bitchez was sitting out front smoking while watching niggaz shoot dice. Lil Coon knew something big was going down, so he parked and got out.

"Lil Bruce and the whole 29Th Terrace was posted up; Lil Bruce was making a bet with some nigga when Lil Coon walked up. "Wuz good big tymin ass nigga?

"Oh, shit," Lil Bruce said, excited to see his nigga.

"Wuz good fam," Lil Bruce gave Lil Coon dap. "You know a nigga tryna live out here in these streets, "Lil Coon looked down.

"Wat you got going on, bruh?" he asked.

"Oh, some Lil nigga wanna race, so I told him to get that Fetti up," Lil Bruce said.

Everybody knew Lil Bruce's brother was the fastest

thing out of Broward County, and anything he ran against lil homie, he always came out on top. This young nigga was only 15-years-old and was paid in full. Lil Bruce and his ol boy Big Bruce won hundreds of thousands of dollars in cash money off his ability to outrun anything that lines up next to him.

"Where dis nigga from? Lil Coon asked, looking confused.

"Which person in their right state of mind wants to race Lil Bruce's brother somewhere in the "Muck City?" Lil Bruce said, shrugging his shoulders.

Because really bruh, it doesn't matter since Lil bruh gonna blow right past him. "How much are they running for? Fifteen thousand dollars...them niggas ain't getting money like that up there in that country ass shit, "Lil Bruce said.

"Everybody was posted up on the long side of 29th, waiting for the youngsters to line up. Lil Bruce stood in the middle of the road while he waited; the whole 29th was swol.

Anytime something like this happens, which it always does, everybody always comes out and places their bets. "Ya'll ready!" Lil Bruce yelled out! Lil Bruce holds up his hands for a few minutes before dropping them.

Lil Bruce's brother took off like a bat out of hell, leaving the youngster looking dumbfounded. Lil Bruce's brother was so fast at the jump that when he took off, the kid knew that he was not going to catch him. He didn't even try. The point has seen money lost.

***

Later That Night
Lil Coon decided to let one of his members open the

club because he had something to handle. Lil Coon was home watching Mayweather, his favorite boxer, when his cell phone started ringing; he grabbed it and answered it. "Hello?"

"The shipment should be there in less than an hour or so. After you take care of business, meet me at the Marriot. I'll be in room 216 and be safe," the other person said before hanging up.

Lil Coon got up from the couch in his living room and walked into his bedroom. Fifteen minutes later, Lil Coon was dressed in all black; he ensured his vest and weapons were secured.

Moments later, Lil Coon was walking out the front door, heading to a van he rented earlier that day. Once he was inside, Lil Coon placed a call just as he was pulling off. Thirty minutes later, Lil Coon was pulling up on Sleep, who was also dressed in all black.

The two made small talk as they drove southbound on I-95 until Lil Coon exited onto Sterling, heading to Dania Beach, where the boats load and unload. It didn't take them long to find where the shipment was taking place.

Lil Coon parked the van from far out of sight and got out with Sleep by his side. Looking at his G-Shock, it read 1:45 AM; they had forty minutes before the boat arrived, so Lil Coon and Sleep checked out the area making sure everything was straight before they got into position and waited.

Forty-five minutes had passed before a speed boat popped up with three Cubans on board and another three standing on the pier. One of the Cubans tied the rope attached to the speed boat, and two of them got on board with the other Cubans.

Lil Coon and Sleep were in the cut watching the Cubans

unload cocaine stuffed in crates; they waited until the Cubans got all the cocaine off the speed boat before striking them, hitting them blindsided.

Lil Coon pulled out his Glock 40 and rushed low; Sleep was by his strap with an A.R 15. Once Lil Coon was close enough, he pointed and fired two shots, killing two Cubans with headshots.

Before the Cubans were able to return, fire and Sleep started spraying, knocking one at a time before throwing their bodies in the water. They wasted no time gathering the crates full of cocaine and loading them into the van; fifteen minutes later, Lil Coon and Sleep were pulling off, jumping back onto I-95.

Once they were back in the hood, Lil Coon and Sleep decided to put the drugs in the stash house, ensuring everything was secure before pulling off.

After Lil Coon and Sleep pulled off and switched vehicles, he made his way to the totel. Finally, after reaching his destination, Lil Coon got out, walked to the elevator, and went to the second floor. Room 216 was a couple of doors down from the elevator; as Lil Coon exited the elevator, he walked towards the room, looking around before knocking. When the room door to the hotel opened, right before his eyes was Myesha, butt-ass naked.

Chapter 21
KILLA

Bray was months away from having their firstborn together; she was having a baby boy, which they both agreed to name after Killa. Bray's weight had picked up tremendously from weighing 130lbs to 175lbs; every chance Bray got, she was eating like a mad woman.

Killa was going shopping twice a week because Bray was eating all the food; all she did was sit her fat ass butt down while she played Candy Crush on her iPhone, demanding food. Ray'anna was always home, so she was the one taking orders like she was a slave.

Killa and Bray's sex life wasn't like before Bray got pregnant. They barely had sex once a week. Killa didn't mind because his love for her was far greater than busting a nut; he was always there for her, even if she just wanted him around.

Their love for each other was priceless, far greater than one can imagine. What could Killa ask for? He was blessed to have a ride-or-die chick who loved him dearly. Killa was a stand-up guy, and from day one, no matter what life threw his way, he managed to throw.

Even without his father being in his life to show him the ropes of life, Killa made the best of every situation and obstacle that came his way. Killa had received a letter from his father two months ago, asking him to sign the papers for visitation. How can a person who has never been in your life just pop up out of the blue and act like everything is supposed to be okay? In Killa's heart, he decided to go through with it even if he didn't want to.

Deep down inside Killa, he loved his father, even if he wasn't present in his life. Rewinding the hands of time when Killa was a Lil boy, memories of his father was good.

Killa was sitting next to Bray in the living room, discussing the matter.

"Bae, I don't know why you are acting like you can't forgive your father," Bray said, eating a bowl of ice cream.

"It ain't I don't forgive him; what I suppose to say when I see him, I don't know dude beside him being my biological father?"

"Bae, you never know; at least feel him out and see what he has to say." Bray knew it was hard for Killa to go through the motions alone, so she supported him any way she could, even if it meant being a shoulder for him to cry.

***

Two Weeks Later

"Sir, could you place your hands on the wall and spread your feet?" a male correction officer demanded of Killa, who really didn't want to be there because it reminded him so much of when he was incarcerated. But he still went along with it for his father's sake.

Once Killa was pat-down searched, the correction officer escorted him to the visitation park, where inmates were sitting with their families. Killa went and took a seat and waited for his father to arrive; less than ten minutes had passed before his father came walking in.

"This nigga looks like me." Killa thought to himself as he stood up for his father to notice him. Soon Killa's father saw him, which wasn't hard because Killa was a split image of him; he smiled while making his way toward the table.

"Hey, son, wuz up?' His father said, looking Killa up and down before giving him a hug.

"Wuz good, pops? Killa responded.

"Look at you all grown up and stuff; the last time I saw you, you were yay high!" his father said, admiring him. "I'm very proud of you, son,."

"Thanks, pops." They both took their seats.

"Wat dey feeding you up in here, you all buffed and shit," Killa asked.

"You got to stay in shape up in here, you know what I'm talking about, right?"

"Yeah, I do Killa said, shaking his head.

A lot of things were running through both of their heads as they were catching up and getting to know each other better. Killa had informed his father about his wonderful child and loving wife, which his father already knew.

The two talked, ate chicken wings, took pictures, and talked about their lives. Killa had to admit that his father was a down-to-earth kind of nigga, and it hurt Killa that his father wasn't ever going to see the streets again.

Unfortunately, Killa was blessed because not only did he walk in his father's shoes, choosing the same path, but he could make it out alive. Killa realized after talking to his father that he couldn't hate him for not being in his life; he played the hand he was dealt.

"Visitation is now over," the officer said over the loud-speaker.

"Well, son, this is it."

"Yeah, pops, Killa stood up and hugged his father.

"Take care out there," you hear me?

"I'ma do that; you just stay strong and hold yourself down."

"I will, son, be easy!" Killa's father gave him a dap and walked to where the other inmates were lining up and walking out of the visitation park.

***

Killa was pulling up in his driveway to the house; his mind was drifting back to the conversation he had with his father. Killa shook it off and exited the vehicle walking toward the front door. Seconds later, Killa entered his home.

"Daddy is home!" he yelled as soon as he stepped in.

"I'm in here, bae!" Bray yelled from the kitchen. Killa walked inside only to find Bray cooking. "Hey, sweetie" How was your visit with your father? "Bray asked, giving him a wet sloppy kiss.

"It was straight," Killa said, opening the refrigerator door before answering. "Something smells good, "Wat is it? Bray turned around with a crab leg in her hand.

"Snow Crabs," she said. All Killa could do was shake his head. Since Bray became pregnant, the only thing she seemed to be doing was eating seafood. Killa sat down at the kitchen table for a minute or two, thinking about his conversation with his father, when Ray'anna entered the kitchen.

"Hey, dad!" Ray'anna said, walking up and hugging Killa.

"Hey baby, Killa embraced her back. Where would Killa be if his daughter wasn't in his life?

"How did it go? Bray said, referring to the visit.

"It was gud, sweetheart," Killa said, looking at Ray'anna to see if there was any resemblance between her and his father.

"Dad… dad, are you alright? Why are you staring at me? Ray'anna said, snapping Killa out of his trance.

"I'm just admiring how beautiful my princess is," Killa said, smiling as he stood up.

"Let me shower so daddy can be ready when dinner is served" Killa walked up and gave Bray and Ray'anna a kiss on their foreheads before walking toward the bedroom. Later that night, Killa and Bray were in bed watching "HITMAN" Killa slid his hands between Bray's legs, feeling all up on her. "Boy! What are you doing?" Bray asked!

"Gurl, stop playing with me; you know what time it is; Killa pulled her panties to the side, and he wasted no time pulling out his dick, easing it in real slow. Bray's pussy was wet like an ocean as he penetrated. "Umm, bae," damn, that shit feels so good," she said, laying on her side.

With every stroke, Killa could feel Bray getting wetter and wetter; just to be on the safe side, Killa had to stop a few times to ensure that her water didn't break. In less than five minutes, Killa was on the verge of climaxing; I guess the saying is true when they say pregnant pussy is the best pussy.

Killa started speeding up, going faster and faster. "Oh shit, I'm finna come" "Oh shit! Was Killa's last words before he busted a nut laying behind Bray, slowly drifting off to sleep.

***

MONEY IS THE ROOT OF ALL EVIL
PERCY

Percy decided to close shop after six months like he said he would, but Wade convinced him to open it back up. Percy did so only on one condition, Wade would take full responsibility, meaning Wade would head.

Percy knew deep down inside the Feds were watching him closely, and it was only a matter of time before it got busted. And when it did, Percy wanted to be far away. Percy was still doing his thing on the low, selling weight, but it was a selected few.

Meanwhile, Percy continued to run the laundry mat staying up under the radar. Percy did explain to Wade that the Feds were watching them and how they worked, but Wade didn't care about all that shit; he saw dollar signs; money is the Root of all Evil.

On Friday night, Lil Coon was throwing a party on 10th Terrace, and everybody was posted up vibing. Percy was trying to call Wade to see if he was coming through, but Wade wasn't picking up for some odd reason.

Hood bitches and niggaz were on both sides of the street watching traffic as it passed. Tonight was Crenshaw on 10th Terrace along with Sunland, the whole hood. Jam Pony Express had the DJ set going on as they played nothing but dirty south music.

Every now and then, a jit would get in the middle of the ride stopping traffic from doing the City Boy dance. Out of the blue, a 73-hard top Donk on 32'S came through doing doughnuts in the middle of the block party, leaving tons of smoke behind.

Nobody knew who was behind the wheel, but whomever it was had something up under the hood that could have been seen from an airplane. Lil Coon, Sleep, and Percy were looking like who the fuck was in the car acting like a straight fool. It only took a matter of time before the driver of the Donk showed his face.

Parking on the side of the street away from everybody, the driver got out. Everybody was surprised when they recognized that person, Wade.

Wade got out with his fat ass blunt hanging from his lips, with a bottle of REMY V.S.O.P in his hand. Wade had everybody's attention, especially Percy. "Ay Ke-Ke! Check it out right quick!" Percy yelled to a chick who was posted up with more hood bitchez.

"Wuz up, baby daddy," Ke-Ke said, walking up and popping her gum. "Gurl, stop playing, but Um, ay" go over where Wade is at and tell him to check it out right quick." With that being said, Ke-Ke walked off in the direction of Wade.

The bottom of Ke-Ke's ass cheeks was hanging out from her short jeans set. Moments later, Ke-Ke was walking back over, swinging her hips from side-to-side. Ke-Ke walked up, rolled her eyes like a real hood rat, standing in her bad bitch stance and said, "Dat nigga told me to tell you to come and holler at him." "Why that nigga acting all sideways and shit?" Percy looked over at Lil Coon, already knowing what he was thinking.

"Don't worry about it, Ke-Ke; bet that up," Percy said, dismissing her. Percy looked over at Sleep. "Ay, Sleep, check me out right," Percy said, walking towards his car. Pre had noticed Wade was acting different since his bankroll started getting fat; everything about Wade changed, and his demeanor and attitude changed, but Percy didn't want to believe it.

Sleep walked over to Percy's vehicle, and they both got up; once Sleep closed the passenger door and looked over at Percy, he noticed that he was in deep thought. "Wuz good homie," you straight, "Sleep said.

"Dawg, this nigga is tripping, bruh! Percy explained the situation to Sleep in the best way he could. Sleep didn't say much about the strength because they were relatives. But if Percy wanted to put Wade to rest, Sleep had no problem.

After Percy finished speaking with Sleep, they both exited the vehicle and walked back to where everybody was, while keeping an eye on Wade.

Around 2:00 am, the block party started thinning out; people started going their separate ways; Wade jumped into his Donk and pulled out into traffic. Percy and the crew stood out front, not too far from the road. Wade made a u-turn and started driving towards Percy and the crew.

Just as Wade was passing by, creeping slow and playing 2 Pac's, "Me Against The World," Wade stopped in front of them and started burning out. Lil Coon looked over at Percy, giving him a look like, nigga if you don't handle him, I will.

***

8:00 AM

Percy was pulling up at the trap with Sleep in the passenger seat; Percy parked and exited his vehicle. Sleep stood out front observing his surroundings, making sure everything was straight.

Percy approached the apartment trap door pulling out an extra set, which of course, he and Wade had. Once walking up to the door, Percy inserted it into the lock, unlocking it; he opened the door and walked in.

Cocaine was scattered all over the table in the front room, a line of rows on top of the line of rows was all Percy saw when he stepped in. What the fuck does Wade have going on? Could he be snorting or fucking with the white girl on the low? This was the only thing going through Percy's head.

Wade wasn't anywhere in sight; just bottles of liquor and rows of cocaine in single lines were the only thing in sight. "Where this nigga at," Sleep asked!

He might be in the room, bruh! Percy responded, walking towards the ajarred room door.

Percy pushed the door open only to find Wade sleeping with two snow bunnies. Cocaine was also next to them, "This explains why Wade started acting funny.

"Wade get your ass up nigga," Percy yelled. Wade jumped up from his sleep, wiping cocaine from his nose. "Are you fucking with that shit nigga? Percy said, pointing to the cocaine.

"Fuck you nigga. I'm a grown-ass man. Who do you suppose to be, my daddy?

Wade got up from between the two snow bunnies, who were butt-ass naked. Percy looked at the situation at hand, knowing Wade was fucking up. "You done bumped your head for real, my nigga" Wade wasn't in his right state of mind, and Percy knew it.

The Feds were watching Percy like a hawk, and then you had Wade tripping and shit. Right then, Percy knew he had to cut his blood off because the stakes were too high, and

Percy didn't want to be Fed bound; he had to cut all ties with Wade.

"Only God can judge me," Wade said, bumping a line of cocaine before passing the mirror that holds the cocaine to one of the girls.

"look nigga I'm going be straight with you, cuz," since I see you on some bomb shit."

"Do you mean because, after today, I ain't fucking with you? "You ain't fucking with me, Naw nigga I ain't fucking with you, you, need me! I put in work 24/7, 365, and look how you treat a nigga.

Wade looked back down at the snow bunnies. "Dat's right! Do you because I'ma do mutherfucki'n me! Wade said, beating on his chest with his fist. Percy looked at Wade one last time before walking out of the room. Fuck this nigga, Percy thought to himself. "Let's ride. "Sleep," Percy said.

CLEAR VISION
KILLA
Chapter 22

Bray was at the Broward General Hospital getting ready to bring her first child into the world; Bray was so happy but still afraid. Killa was right there in the delivery room by her side, encouraging her that everything would be okay.

Bray was in a whole lot of pain, and she lay in bed pushing, but it seemed like the pain wasn't going away. Tears were rolling down Bray's face as she tried her hardest to follow the doctor's instructions and push.

I fucking hate you; I fucking hate you, "Bray said, looking over at Killa as she pushed and pushed.

"It's coming, keep pushing," the doctor said, reaching his hand into Bray's vagina, finally pulling her baby free.

The labor lasted for three hours, and Bray was weak; she had never experienced anything so painful in her life other than giving birth. Before the doctors and nurses were able to clean the baby off, Bray was fully asleep.

Moments later, when she woke up, she was surrounded by family and friends; Mr. Roberts was holding baby Keith and thanking God for his many blessings. Killa was so happy Bray had brought his first son into the world; words couldn't express it.

K-Dog, Lil Coon, Sleep, Percy, and the whole Take Over family were there giving presents. Pictures were taken with them holding Baby Keith one at a time.

Around 10:45 pm, Bray was allowed to go home with her baby, which was a good thing because Bray didn't want to be there any longer than she had to.

***

Since giving birth to her first child, Bray couldn't stop posting pictures on Facebook. Every chance she got, Bray was posting pictures of her son. Giving birth was a dream Bray thought would never come true.

Even Ray'anna was so excited about having a baby brother that she started helping with the baby a lot, and Killa liked this because him and Bray enough time to catch up on their sex life. Every day, they made sweet love. The only time they came out of the room was if something important came up.

Bray was lying in bed next to Killa when she woke up and felt him between her legs; it felt like Bray had wet herself up. She looked over to find Killa sleeping; she reached under the cover, grabbing Killa's semi-hard dick.

"Bae, I want some," Bray said, climbing on top of Killa and waking him up. "What time is it?" he asked.

"It doesn't matter. I'm hot and want sum." Without waiting for an answer, Bray grabbed his dick as Killa layed their butt-naked and slid him into her juices.

Bray started riding Killa, bouncing herself up and down, making her ass cheeks shake; Bray's ass and breasts had gotten bigger, so she could throw down a lil better.

119

Killa was enjoying every minute of it as Bray slow fucked him; this sex was mind-blowing. Just as they were on the verge of climaxing, Lil Keith started crying, breaking their concentration.

"Damn," Bray yelled out.

"See what you did, girl?" Killa said, slapping her on the butt.

"Shut up"! Bray got up, putting on her robe. "I'll be right back," Bray said, walking out of the room.

***

Killa was sitting in a brand new X6 BMW at the car lot on the showroom floor; he was thinking about his future: twenty years from now and where he would be. Life was good; he was still young and had a bank account one would kill for.

While Killa was thinking about the shit he'd been through, K-Dog came walking up in his business attire and broke Killa out of his train of thought. "Wuz good bruh, Wuz on your mind,?"

"Aww man, life dawg," Killa responded.

"Thinking about the future, I bet twenty years from now."

"I guess you read my mind because that's exactly what I was thinking" Killa looked into K-Dog's eyes.

"Aye, bruh, you ever thought about where we would have been if we never ran down on pimp? "Killa asked.

"We would have come up with something. Killa, you remember what I said when we opened that safe that night?"

"Yeah, I remember, bruh! How could I forget that night my whole life changed?" Killa thought about the night they became young, rich niggaz.

"What I said, bruh?" K-Dog asked.

"You said we were blessed," Killa said, looking at K-Dog sitting in the BMW. "Don't ever forget it!" K-Dog reached into the vehicle patting Killa on the shoulder before walking off, leaving him to think.

In For a Surprise
K-Dog
Chapter 23

This was Lil Coon's second time running down on people who's powerful, if not more powerful than the Take Over Family. K-Dog had to clean up Lil Coon's mess the first time with Zoe Pound; now, he turned right around and hit the Cuban Cartel.

This was some serious shit, especially regarding the Cuban Cartel; these motherfuckers are very dangerous and ruthless. Word got back to K-Dog yesterday that Myesha's dude is not only her man, but he is second in command of the Cuban Cartel.

K-Dog wanted to hear what Lil Coon had to say, so he called him up. Twenty minutes later, Lil Coon was walking through K-Dog's front door dressed in a white tailor-made line suit. Lil Coon walked up to K-Dog and embraced him like a son would his father.

"Wuz up, old timer," Lil Coon said, as he stepped back and examined him. "I'm good young blood K-Dog walked towards his office, telling Lil Coon to follow.

Dominique and the kids were upstairs playing board games. That's where K-Dog wanted them. Once K-Dog entered the room, he sat behind his large oakwood desk. Lil Coon came in also before closing the door behind them.

K-Dog looked at Lil Coon for a minute, trying to see what this nigga was thinking about, but he wanted to know where his head was at. Lil Coon felt that K-Dog wanted to speak to him about the hit him and Sleep did.

The only difference between Zoe Pound and the Cuban Cartel was that Lil Coon had this situation under control. Reading Lil Coon's mind was like running into a brick wall. K-Dog knew Lil Coon was unpredictable, so he gave up and let Lil Coon know what was on his mind.

***

If anybody knew him, everything about K-Dog, one could say that he's a businessman. K-Dog went through a lot of shit, fighting to get to the top, and it wasn't easy. Years later, K-Dog built a strong team from the bottom, along with Killa's help.

K-Dog wasn't the type to get into people's personal life, especially when it came down to his members. But that damn Lil Coon was another fucking story.

K-Dog knew he had to stay on top of Lil Coon because if he didn't, Lil Coon would have the whole Take Over Family going to war, dealing with the Percy situation, and getting jammed up with the Alphabet Boys.

Let's be honest, damn near every dope boy or another had gotten involved with the law enforcers in some fashion. This was the shit that K-Dog was thinking about as he drove to Cinnamon's place; the whole time K-Dog was en route, he was smoking that purp, listening to 2Pac's, "Dear Mama."

.

Twenty minutes later, he was pulling up to the house he had brought for Cinnamon, parking behind her BMW Coup; K-Dog exited the vehicle making his way towards the front door. Out of the blue, Cinnamon's neighbor pulled up on a lawn mower along side his fence and called him.

Mr. Lynch was an old, retired policeman. "How you been, Mr. Lynch," K-Dog said!

"I'm good, son! Mr. ersaid. Turning off his lawn mower, Mr. Lynch said, "I know you haven't forgotten about me, have you, son?"

"Come on, Mr. Lynch, you know I ain't forget about you"! K-Dog reached into his pocket, pulled out a sandwich bag full of weed, and gave it to him. Mr. Lynch cuffed it before his wife saw it.

"Thank you, Son. Now I can roll up and smoke one; that's how I can put up with my wife. When I'm high, I pay her no attention, "Mr. Lynch laughed to himself.

"Tom! Mr. Lynch's wife called for him, and soon she walked out the front door oftheir house.

"See, this is the shit I'm talking about," Mr. Lynch turned on his lawn mower again.

"See you, Son," he said, pulling off; all K-Dog could do was shake his head as he made his way to the front door.

Cinnamon and Season were in the middle of the front door getting their freak on; Cinnamon was lying on her back while her legs were wide open, and Season was eating her out.

K-Dog wasted no time stripping out of his clothes before getting behind Season, who had her ass up in the air as she gave Cinnamon the best head ever. Once K-Dog was in position, he inserted his dick inside Season's sweet garden from the back.

The three of them went at it for an hour, straight fucking and sucking each other like they were porn stars. After getting their freak on, the three of them lay on the floor drenched. K-Dog didn't know he was in for a surprise that would change his life forever.

Cinnamon reached over and fondled with K-Dog's dick as he lay with both girls on each side of him; Cinnamon was trying to figure out how she was going to reveal to K-Dog their secret. Cinnamon looked over at Season, giving her the eye that it was time. Then Season gave her the thumbs up.

"Papi?"

"Yeah, wuz up, we have something to tell you!" Cinnamon said K-Dog had his eyes closed as Cinnamon continued to caress his balls.

"I'm listening. You can tell me anything," K-Dog said, reaching over and grabbing Cinnamon's nipple.

"Papi, we pregnant, me and Season!" Cinnamon blurted out.

K-Dog opened his eyes and looked at them like it was a dream and not reality.

Chapter 24
PERCY

After witnessing how Wade was fucking around with the white girl, Percy stopped dealing with him. Wade's true colors started to show every other day. Wade would post something about Percy on Facebook.

Saying Percy was working with the Feds creating problems that he wasn't ready for. On the strength, since Wade was family, Percy decided that he would be the bigger man and not feed into Wade's bullshit.

One night while Percy was chilling inside Club Dungeon, Wade walked in with other niggas acting like he was on some bossed-up shit. This nigga was disrespectful by grabbing all up on them, disregarding the rules.

Word had got back to Lil Coon, who was itching to put a bullet right between Wade's eyes. Lil Coon exited his office with Sleep and a few of his hitters; Percy looked up just in time to see what was about to jump off.

"SHIT!" The person said as he got up and walked to where Wade and his niggaz were and tried to talk some sense into him before Lil Coon walked up.

"Wat the fuck wrong with you nigga?" Lil Coon asked, looking deep into Wade's eyes.

"Don't you know that shit will get you killed" What? Nigga are you ready to die? Die! Shit, the only thing I'm worried about is money; that other shit is irrelevant! Lil Coon couldn't believe what he was; before he could react, Shavon stepped in.

"Wade... Boy, what you got going on? I don't know what's gotten into you lately that got you acting like dis! But you need to please stop." Shavon was trying to talk some sense into Wade's head because she knew how it was going to end, blood or not, it was gonna end in a bloody tragedy.

"What you need to do is get the fuck out of my face bitch, before I..." Before he could finish his sentence, Percy punched him dead in the jaw knocking Wade to the floor. The niggas with Wade pulled out guns and pointed them at Lil Coon and the rest of his crew.

"What the fuck!" Lil Coon couldn't believe these lame ass niggas were pointing guns at him in his establishment. "Bae go head and leave," Lil Coon said to Shavon, not taking his eyes off the dudes.

Shavon walked away. There wasn't anything she could have done; she tried her best! And now it was out of her hands. Lil Coon waited for Shavon to leave before he started speaking.

"Ya'll be got to the count of ten to leave before dis shit hit the fan." By this time, security guards surrounded them with AK'S. "And five of them are already gone; they knew they were outnumbered, and it was a Loose! Loose! Situation. So, they lowered their weapons.

"Now get the fuck out nigga! Before I change my mind!" Lil Coon made it clear that he was playing for keeps. The best thing to do was leave and live to fight another day, but little did they know that night was the last night they would ever see any ass or pussy again.

No Understanding...
Lil Coon
Chapter 25

Lil Coon was sitting in his office alone, thinking about how he was going to deliver Wade's fate. Shavon walked in and tried to talk to Lil Coon. "Baby, you know that's my cousin, and I don't want nothing to happen to him."

"I understand that, boo, that's why he's not already dead."

I truly thought about it," Lil Coon said, placing his right hand over his heart. Shavon thought about it before coming up with an idea.

"Alright, bae, if anything happens to Wade, I'll feel much better if Percy would handle it and not you."

Shavon knew Wade had fucked up big time, so she walked out of the office and caught up with Wade who was outside in the parking lot. Shavon informed Wade that his life was in jeopardy, she offered him $20,000 in cash to leave, but of course, he refused. And for that, Wade would have to pay for it with his life.

***

5:20 AM Later That Night... I

Across the street from Denny's, where Wade and his crew were eating, Lil Coon, Sleep, and Percy sat in the cut. Wade didn't know nor had any idea what was waiting on him until it was too late. "Dere they go, bruh" they are coming out now, "Sleep said" sitting in the driver seat of the vehicle.

"Percy, don't play with Dez niggaz; all of them gotta go, Lil Coon said," cocking his 223 back. Percy made it clear what he had to do. He cocked his AR15, looking up from the back seat.

"Let's do this Percy said with death written all over him. They watched as Wade and his crew walked out of Denny's and got into Wade's vehicle; moments later, they were pulling out on Davie in the middle of traffic.

Sleep pulled out behind the fourth vehicle in traffic and followed them until they stopped at the four-way on 34th and Parkway; Sleep eased the car alongside of Wade's vehicle as Lil Coon and Percy were hanging out window, sticks already drawn.

Before Wade and his homies realized what had hit them, bullets were flying; 223s and 7.62s started knocking holes inside Wade's vehicle, bullets penetrating from one end of the vehicle and exiting out from the other side.

Percy hurried up, jumping out with his Choppa in his hand, running over to Wade's Donk and snatching the car door open. Without any hesitation, Percy wasted no time pointing his stick at Wade and and leavingsqueezed the trigger, killing them all before jumping back into the waiting vehicle, pulling off behind dead bodies.

***

After Lil Coon, Sleep, and Percy ran down on Wade, Lil Coon went to this bad bitch's house name Abla. Ms. USA didn't have shit on Abla; she was bad, and Alba was a super-fly, bossed-up bitch. When Lil Coon got to her house, he got out and walked towards the front door knocking.

Lil Coon waited, thinking to himself what he was going to say when Alba opened the front door. Seconds later, the door opened, and there she stood, looking like she had come straight from heaven.

"Damn, Lil Coon said to himself, as he looked Alba up and down; slim redbone, long hair doesn't care; every man's dream, and there she was standing right there in front of Lil Coon.

Alba knew by the looks of it that Lil Coon had got into something or done something; without saying a word, Alba turned around and walked towards her bedroom, leaving Lil Coon. "SHIT," he said under his breath as he closed the door.

The last time Lil Coon showed up at Alba's house at this morning, he had flipped the Haitians from Zoe Pound. Lil Coon knew Alba felt some way about him and that she had strong feelings for him , but the lifestyle he was living was the only thing that kept them from being together.

Lil Coon also had a thing or two for Alba; it's been like this ever since he laid eyes on Alba back in the day. But he couldn't give Alba all of him since he was involved with Shavon. Once Lil Coon closed and locked the front door, he walked into Alba's bedroom only to find her lying in her panties.

Lil Coon stripped down to his boxers and got into the

bed easing up behind Alba. "Wuz good ma? "Lil Coon said," smelling her hair.

"I'm a good daddy! Alba said, backing her ass up on Lil Coon's dick. Alba knew Lil Coon was a straight hitter and didn't mind sending niggas home early, and his lifestyle went against everything she was taught.

But Alba continued to fuck with Lil Coon. Why? Because this nigga was a motherfucker. "Coon" want some Alba! Please! Pulling him closer to her.

"You miss me, sexy? Lil Coon asked, planting kisses on the back of her neck and positioning himself on her backside.

"Boy, what type of question is that? You know I miss this dick." Lil Coon slid Alba's panties to the side, rubbing his dick between and up and down the crack of her ass, before sliding his dick into Alba's pretty pink pussy.

***

Days Later …

Lil Coon was on top of the building, watching his target through a sniper rifle. Myesha had given Lil Coon the time and place where her boyfriend would be; it just so happened that it was a restaurant.

Lil Coon watched the target as he sat by the window inside the restaurant reading the Daily newspaper. Out front far were two bodyguards not too far from a parked limousine, talking to each other, not knowing their boss was sitting between crosshairs.

While the target was reading the newspaper, a waitress walked up to take his order when, out of the blue right before her eyes, she witnessed his brains getting knocked out everywhere.

"OH MY GOD!" the waitress yelled. Blood and brains were all over the waitress's face and uniform. The sight alone was horrifying; just witnessing tragedy upfront like that, the waitress dropped to her knees and started screaming.

Lil Coon hurried and broke down his rifle, securing it before walking down a flight of stairs. Once on ground level, Lil Coon looked around, seeing how everybody was losing their minds. MISSION COMPLETE

Taking one last look, Lil Coon turned and walked off, attending to his everyday business… CHECKMATE… GAME OVER.

CAUGHT OFF GUARDS
Killa
Chapter 26

Diamond was spending more of her time at school at the Y.M.C.A. and the park. Just being around individuals playing chess, Diamond had enough time on her hands to develop not only the means to play but also a complex strategy that had everybody in awe.

One day while Diamond was at the park, she walked under the pavilion where Killa and a few members were playing chess. Diamond walked up, observing them closely and listening as they talked about the game's rules.

"Hey ya'll" Diamond said, interrupting them.

"Wuz up? Baby girl," one of the members, said, looking at her. "When I get big and old enough, I'ma show ya'll how to get to the top, watch and see." Diamond said with her hands on her hips.

Hearing Diamond talk like this wasn't anything new to them, especially to Killa. It ran deep in Diamond's blood; she wanted to be just like her father whether her mother approved of it or not.

"And how you are going to do that, Baby girl," another member asked.

"Easy, my brotha." is all I need, like chess "you know how to play chess, right?

"Yeah," they all said in union, wanting to hear what she had to say.

Alright then, but it's going be the other way around; instead of the king being priceless, I'ma take that position and be the mastermind. And my brotha, where is he?" Diamond asked, looking for her brother calling his name.

"J-Money!" she yelled loud enough for him to hear. Diamond waited until he came. She placed her hand on J-Money's shoulder. "Now, like I was saying, um, where was I?" Diamond said to herself, looking up.

"Oh yeah," I'ma, be the mastermind, and my brotha gonna be the muscle. In no time, we are going to take over and finish what my father started," Diamond looked over at Killa "And you Uncle Keith, ain't that right J-Money?

All he could do was shake his head because he had already witnessed how smart Diamond was. Regardless of if they took her seriously or not, they would see that Diamond meant every word.

"It's been nice talking with ya'll, but I got a chess game to play with my mentor," Diamond said, pointing under the tree where Lil Coon was sitting. "Until we meet again, ya'll stay out of trouble." Ready to go, she said, "J-Money, let's go!

Diamond turned and walked off with her brother behind her. Killa replayed what Diamond said about her being the mastermind and J-Money being the muscle. Looking back, ever since Diamond was born, she stayed under her father every chance she got, soaking up everything like a sponge.

Diamond never hung out with kids her age; it's always been older folks she surrounded herself around most of the time. Sunland Park was a recreational center place where people could come at any time or day and chill, smoke a blunt, or come through the late night with a chick.

Killa had rebuilt it, making it a lovely park to hang at, despite all the hood shit that surrounded it. Killa was walking through the park hollering at a few niggas, keeping it gangsta; the kids out playing ran up, giving him hugs.

This nigga was changing people's lives, bringing heaven right to the earth. Off to the side, by the pool area, was a hut, where everybody hung out, was a group of people smoking weed and playing spades.

Killa walked up all fresh and shit, designer down with his neck and wrist iced out. "Wat dey do homie?" One of the dudes in the crowd said, giving Killa a dap.

" You already know Lil One...Another day, another dollar," Killa responded as he walked up to every one of them, giving them dap.

This redbone playing spades reminded him of this chick he used to know, but that was back in the day. "Who got next?" Killa asked.

"You! Because dez some trash bitchez," Lil One said, slamming a winning card down.

"Nigga you trash, at least I count all 52 cards, and not just sometime spades," the redbone said, making everybody laugh, including Killa. Lil One was out of S.C. Kingstree, born and raised; even though he wasn't from the south, you would've thought he was.

Lil One had that Lauderdale swag down to an essence. While everybody tried to shit, Killa was trying to remember where he knew this bad redbone. Then out of the blue, it hit him like a ton of bricks; now he remembered.

Back when Killa was seventeen, he ran down on her at a block party when she was with her friends. Killa and K-Dog had a few homies; they all got together and went to the hotel.

Killa was caught in his train of thought that he didn't hear his name being called. "Killa you wanna play bruh?" Lil One asked for the second time.

"Huh...Oh...naww, Lil homie, I'm good to do your thing. I'm good," Killa said.

The redbone got up from the table, grabbing her phone and keys. "Alright, y'all take care! the she said.

"I'll see you later, gurl," another chick said. Killa looked as she walked off before asking the girl a question.

"Ay ain't her name Lee-Lee?

"Yep, that's her; the girl responded, looking Killa up and down. "Why?" She asked. Killa didn't say a word; he took off after her.

"Excuse me," Killa said," walking up to her. Lee-Lee right"

"Yes, that's me," Lee-Lee said, turning around.

"Long time no see stranger; how have you been doing?"

"I've been doing good, and by the way, you the stranger!

"And what makes you say that?" Killa asked, , focusing on her body. DAMN! He thought.

Lee-Lee is bad, Killa thought to himself. .

"It's you that never noticed me until now." Killa and Lee-Lee were talking about the last encounter together when suddenly, Lee-Lee hit Killa with a low blow catching him off guard. "I know it's been a long time since we've talked; Lee-Lee paused for a moment, thinking to herself before continuing. "The last encounter we had together, you remember, right?

"Of course...How could I not remember," Killa said, thinking about the last time. 17 to 18 years old, "We'll you've given me something to call my own."

"Call yo own, what's that supposed to mean?

Killa was looking confused. What in the world was Lee referring to. Lee-Lee braced herself to get ready to recite what she had rehearsed for the past sixteen years after realizing her son didn't belong to her boyfriend.

This meant her baby was no other than Killa's. Lee-Lee knew there was no turning back; she had him right where she wanted him. Lee-Lee took a deep breath and let the words roll right off her tongue. "You've given me a son.

Heart Crushed
K-Dog
Chapter 27

A lot of shit was going through K-Dog's head as he laid next to Dominique; not only did he get Cinnamon pregnant, but Season as well. How in the hell was K-Dog going to explain this to Dominique, the woman he made his wife?

After all they have been through together, and accomplished over the years, Dominique has been standing strong by K-Dog's side. Would this ruin everything they fought so hard to keep together? If Dominique ever found out, would she woman up, keep her word, and leave him for good?

While K-Dog was thinking, his phone started ringing, snapping him back to reality. "Hey Papi, I was wondering can you come over? I was getting lonely," Cinnamon said, as her English improved.

K-Dog looked over at Dominique, who was reading her urban book by K'wan. "Give me a minute. I'm on my way." K-Dog hung up. "What book are you reading now?" K-Dog asked, kissing Dominique.

"Hood Rat Chicks by K'wan," she replied.

"Ain't that the dude out of New York?" K-Dog asked, getting out the bed and walking to the bathroom.

"Yep, that's him," Dominique said as she reached and grabbed his cell; while K-Dog was using the bathroom, Dominique was going through his phone.

She read the text messages between Cinnamon and Season. Dominique couldn't believe what she was seeing. Tears started falling from her eyes as she read all 300-plus messages.

Dominique hurriedly wiped away her tears as she heard the toilet being flushed. K-Dog stepped out of the bathroom, put on his shoes and clothes, and grabbed his cell phone before hitting the door.

***

Later that night, K-Dog was pulling up in the driveway to find Dominique's car missing. It was 12:43 am, and she wasn't there. Where in the world could Dominique be? This was the only thing on K-Dog's mind was as he entered the front door.

No lights were on, and the whole house was totally quiet; K-Dog walked into their master bedroom, turning on the lights. Dominique was no were to be found. On the dresser was a piece of paper folded out in plain view; K-Dog grabbed it and opened it; to his surprise, it was a handwritten letter from Dominique.

"MOTHER EARTH"

She hurt because you made her feel like the dirt on this Earth that people walk all over and take advantage of without loving anything she does. She nourishes, provides, protects, and is always around. She hates that you get her down and turn her smile into frowns. She is ready for love to grow in her heart and for it to never stop. She doesn't have to have the white picket fence, just a man with a good sense of how to be a good man, a good father, a good friend, and a wonderful protector. She is like the wind that tickles your body and runs her hands through your hair, but you do not see this as a sign that she cares. She is playful as she turns you around and round and whispers in your ear without making a sound. She is fierce like fire for your every desire, and she even calls you sire. You dare not acknowledge her with respect; she should get for all she does for you. "Why should you regret it? You should respect her and cherish her, for there wouldn't be no you without her; she is your Mother Earth. Just like a tornado, she may seem confused and throw blows that feel like hail, she may cry as heaven rain, she may get as loud as a train on the tracks, but if you could see her eyes, you'll see there's hope. There's calm within this storm; remember, just as the soil must be turned and handled gently to bring life, so does this woman that has so many characteristics as Mother Earth.   D.SHAW

After K-Dog finished reading Dominique's letter, he rushed out of the room and ran into J-Money's room. EMPTY. "DAMN!" K-Dog said out loud. He went into Diamond's room; it was also empty. K-Dog had to sit down and think because this shit couldn't be real; why did Dominique just up and leave a nigga taking the clothes and all?

K-Dog thought to himself. He pulled his phone out of his pocket and called Dominique. "Who is she? And don't lie because I read all 300 and something messages between you, Cinnamon, and Season." Dominique yelled at the top of her lungs, mad as hell.

K-Dog shot straight into mode. "Hold up! First you violated by going through my shit, then you leave a nigga, taking my kids and all without talking about the matter like two adults." K-Dog started pacing around the large house, trying to cool down.

It wasn't Dominique leaving that had him 38-hot; it was the fact she took the kids away. They are his world, his pride, and joy, his everything, and she got the nerves to take them away from him.

"My kids is all I got. They keep me alive, breathing to see another day." "Don't do me like this, Molly, please!"

"What do you want me to do? Just accept the fact that my husband is having an affair with two bitchez."

"I'm not asking you shit, Molly; at least come home so we can talk this shit through."

"K-Dog's head was spinning; he was trying to get control of his feelings and emotions. "You wanna know what I would have done?" K-Dog asked.

"Yes, I wanna know."

"First off, I wouldn't just up and leave without addressing the situation.

"I love you too much to walk outta yo life, and if I did catch you cheating, I would still love you and be by your side. Baby can't no woman compare to you or come between what we established, and I mean that on my kid's life," K-Dog stopped for a minute letting the words sink in.

"Baby, I'm not perfect in any shape or form, but I know I'll climb the highest mountain. I'll swim the deepest ocean to be with you. Molly, look all I am saying in so many words, baby, I'm human." K-Dog was speaking from the essence of his heart.

Dominique was furious. It hurt her dearly that K-Dog

didn't deny the allegations. Regardless of how much she loved him, she couldn't bring herself to overlook that her man was cheating.

"Kenny, look;. I need time to get my head clear because I honestly don't know what I wanna do. But Um, if you wanna see the kids, I don't have a problem, they'll be at my mother's." Tears were falling down Dominique's eyes; it was only one word to how she was feeling, BETRAYED. "I'm sorry, but I have to go, Kenny."

"Hold up, Molly, Molly shit!" Dominique ended the call.

Well, I'll Be Damn...
Killa
Chapter 28

Killa had other problems to deal with, like the fact that he had a child and didn't know anything about it. Today would be the first time seeing him. He wondered if the kid was his in the first place. This was the only thing going through Killa's head as he was driving to Lee-Lee's place.

North Lauderdale was a nice neighborhood mostly surrounded by whites and Mexicans. When Killa pulled up in the Lee-Lee's driveway, he called her. Moments later, Lee-Lee walked out her front door with a teenage boy that looked identical to Killa.

"Damn," Killa said to himself as he exited the Range Rover.

"Keith, I would like for you to meet Trey, and Trey, this is Keith, your father," Lee-Lee said, introducing the two. They both looked at one another from head to toe. Killa was staring Trey down, and Trey was doing the same.

"Killa," Trey said, looking over at his mother. "Dis my Ole Boy, you kiddin me right? Do you know who this nigga is?

"Yes, boy, I know who he is."

"Dis nigga got the whole world in his hands. "And now you letting me know this after all this time and years that this is my father?"

Trey said, pointing at Killa with a stern face, "OH SHIT, POPS, WUZ UP"! Trey was happy smiling ear to ear, spreading out his arms as he walked towards Killa, giving him a bear hug.

Killa and Trey were caught in the moment, enjoying the father and son's affection; Lee-Lee stood there with tears in her eyes. If she knew they would both act like this, she would have made this happen, Lee-Lee would've overlooked her feelings and emotions, and how she felt about the situation it made Trey and Killa happy. By the looks of it, Lee-Lee automatically knew that they would get along together.

"Ya'll gud right?" Lee-Lee asked.

"Yeah, ma we gud; we just need a lil time together, dat's all." Trey looked over at Killa for him to put his two cents in. Killa smiled because he peeped at how Trey was handling the situation and liked it.

"Yeah, we gud Red I got him," Killa said, calling Lee-Lee the nickname he gave her back in the days.

"You got a license?" Killa asked Trey. "Get in and drive." Killa walked up and kissed Lee-Lee on the cheek before walking towards the passenger seat.

"Take care of my baby Keith... he's all I got!" Lee-Lee yelled as Trey was backing out of the driveway.

***

When Killa and Trey walked through the front door, Ray'anna was sitting on the couch watching B.E.T. Bringing Trey to see his sister and brother at Killa's house was the best day of Ray'anna's life because when she saw Trey, Ray'anna automatically knew that he was her brother.

When Ray'anna saw both father and son, she thought she saw doubles. Ray'anna jumped up from the sofa, stood in front of them both, and just looked at them; finally, she said. "Hey, bruh, wuz up?" Ray'anna reached out her hand.

"My name is Ray'anna, and what's yours?"

"Trey...y name is Trey," he responded. Shaking hands with Ray'anna,

"It's nice to meet you; where have you been?" Ray'anna curiously asked. Before Trey responded, he looked over at Killa and shrugged his shoulders.

"I been around."

"Dad, you never informed me that I had a big brother," Ray'anna said.

"Dat's because I just found out?"

"We'll see... what do you think mom is going to say when she finds out?"

"I don't know," Killa responded.

"Find out what?" Bray asked, as she walked into the living room with Lil Keith in her arms. Bray looked at Trey, then at Killa; she was shocked.

"Bae dis is Trey," Killa said, walking up to Bray and taking his son from his mother's grip.

"I'm speechless; Kenny, ya'll go for twins." Then, Bray asked, "How old is he?".

"He'll be sixteen in a couple of months." Bray did the numbers in her head and knew whoever Trey's mom was, it was before her time.

Bray was happier than anything as they sat down and talked; Killa explained everything to her, not leaving anything out.

Killa didn't know that Trey was a member of a, well-know click, known as the Jack Boys. This group of thugs was known for one thing, gunplay. Getting money off robbing niggaz was what Trey and his homies did for a living; since Trey was fifteen, he was in the streetz, headfirst.

Sunday 1:15 PM

Trey was riding in his Lexus Coup Killa gave him a week ago, smoking a fat blunt with a redbone in the seat. Trey had just turned onto 3rd Avenue off Sunrise and pulled up to a trap house; before getting out of his vehicle, Trey looked around, observing his surroundings before exiting.

"Blow the horn twice if shit starts to look funny," Trey said to the redbone as he exited his Lexus Coup.

"I got you, daddy; just be careful. With that being said, Trey closed the driver's door and walked towards the front door and knocked. Seconds later, the door opened, and some nigga was standing there looking like he was geeked up on Molly's. "Wuz gud bruh? The dude said, looking Trey up and down.

"Let me get a dirt bike" (4 ½ ounces of cocaine), Trey responded, looking like he had just come from the jeweler.

Trey knew he had to look like a dope boy instead of a jack boy to complete the mission, a perfect disguise. "Come on in, homie, I got cha." The dealer let Trey in, not knowing what his intentions were until it was too late.

Trey saw that it was only him in the trap and nobody else; easy money, he thought to himself. Trey waited to see where the drugs were before pulling out his throwaway, pointing it at the dude's head. "Damn," the dealer said after realizing he got caught slipping.

In less than five minutes, Trey was walking out the door, smooth as a whistle, with a book bag stuffed with money and drugs. Trey opened the driver's door and threw the book bag on the back seat; then he got in and pulled off.

"You got her thang, daddy?"

"You damn right I did," Trey said, heading up towards Six-Trunk. "I told you he was loaded the redbone said.

Too Much Blood Shedding...
Percy
Chapter 29

Percy couldn't sleep as he layed next to Pre; it was like Pimp's face was hunting him every time he closed his eyes. Pimp's face was in plain view. The promise he made about killing the person who killed his father was fucking with him bad. Not only did Percy know who took his father from him, but he was affiliated with the nigga; he wanted to kill K-Dog. If it weren't for K-Dog, Percy wouldn't be where he was at today, let alone accomplish the things he had thus far: a big house, a laundromat, and six figures; Percy was living off interest because everything he had was paid for.

Truth be told, regardless of how K-Dog did for Percy, he just didn't feel right. Something had to give, even if it cost him his life; Percy had to figure this shit out.

***

Wade was lying in the casket at James Boyd's funeral home, off Six-Trunk and 22nd Avenue. Family and friends were getting ready to load up in the limousines out front, and all of them walked out.

Percy, Shavon, Lil Coon, and Pre were seated in the front seats of the limousine, while the rest of the family got into the others. Once the limousine was full, they all headed to the House of God for the service.

Forty-five minutes later, Pastor Roberts opened the ceremony once everybody was seated. Her speech was powerful as always. "Another child has been put to rest at an early age. When is the black-on-black killing gonna stop," Pastor Roberts looked over the whole church at all 1,500 people before setting her eyes on Shavon.

"Lord, help us all because we need you right now, Jesus! If it's not the white folks killing, then it's us killing each other." Pastor Roberts' words has touched Shavon so bad it caused her to break down. Because the thought of her knowing she had something to do with the murder convicted her.

The whole church had to be put on hold because of how bad Shavon was. Percy and Lil Coon had to tote Shavon on their shoulders outside the limo.

"We are responsible. Oh God... we are responsible," were the words Shavon kept screaming from the limo. Shavon was losing her mind; her mom had to get her medical help, so they transported her to Broward General Medical Center for treatment.

Broward General refused to treat Shavon because she needed mental help, so they transferred her ass to the crazy house. The family had to sit and wait until the doctors allowed them to see her.

Just to let you know, Shavon is under a lot of pressure now, but with the medication we have her on, well let's just say we'll have her back in no time. God willing." The doctor said that in front of Lil Coon and the whole family.

"What the fuck is that supposed to mean? God willing," Lil Coon said, getting all up in the doctor's face, sending chills through his body. Shavon's mother had to get between them to defuse the situation, which was a good thing because moments later, they were walking inside the room.

Whatever medication they had Shavon on, she slept like a newborn baby. Everybody stood around Shavon looking like, Damn, I can't believe this shit is happening.

"Dawg, this shit ain't real, bruh!" Percy said, breaking the silence in the room. Everybody stared and prayed, hoping for the best and not the worst because what they were seeing was a fucked up look for Shavon.

Shavon woke up looking at the faces. "Who you?" Shavon asked before she started screaming and hollering to the top of her lungs while pulling her hair with both hands.

"Doctor, Doctor, Doctor!!!" Lil Coon yelled out, panicking, because seeing Shavon out of her mind began to fuck with his. The Doctors and nurses rushed into the room well-prepared; they went right over to Shavon and grabbed her; they were not playing at all. I'm talking about excessive force. Shavon was bucking like a wild animal out of control. The scene looked like it was supposed to be in a horror movie.

"Everybody get the fuck out of the room now," some big ass medical staff rushed in and spoke.

"You'll get ya'll hand off my girl," Lil Coon yelled out, as they rushed everybody out of the room.

"Sir, I need you all to please leave the room so we can take care of the situation at hand." Just as the room door closed, Lil Coon saw Shavon as she snatched the needles out of her arms.

It wasn't anything he could've done that would've made the situation better. "Damn," Lil Coon said as the door closed.

***

Wade is dead, Shavon is in the crazy house, losing her damn mind, and Percy is starting to feel some way. THIS THE NIGGA THAT KILLED MY OLE BOY AND TOOK HIM AWAY FROM ME... Percy kept replaying in his head over and over again; for the last week, all Percy had been doing was drinking alcohol by the 5ths.

Even Pre knew something wasn't right with Percy; something was heavy on his mind because whatever it was, it had Percy's heart turning cold. It didn't matter what it took for Percy to fulfill the promise he made to himself; he would lose his life in the process.

Love is Pain
Lil Coon
Three Weeks Later...
10:35 AM
Chapter 30

Lil Coon was pulling up to the facility where they were housing Shavon; today was visiting hours for her, so Lil Coon decided to slide through to see what the fuck was up. Once parking his AUDI A8, Lil Coon got out of the vehicle dressed like he deserved to be on the cover of Source Magazine.

As he entered the building, Lil Coon walked over to the front desk. "I'm here to see Shavon Love," Lil Coon said to the receptionist.

"Have a seat, and somebody will be with you shortly," she said, looking like Ms. Piggy.

Without saying a word, Lil Coon walked over and took a seat in the waiting room; he waited a whole hour before he was allowed to see Shavon. An old fat white lady, straight trailer trash walked up in front of Lil Coon, dressed in a full white nurse's outfit, with the hat and all.

"Are you here to visit Ms. Love?"

"Yes, mam," Lil Coon responded.

"Follow me this way. The nurse lady led Lil Coon through a set of double doors, entering a room with crazy people.

Lil Coon had to stop for a moment and look around for a while because what he saw looked like a walking dead show." THESE PEOPLE LOOK LIKE ZOMBIES, Lil Coon said in his head.

"She's over here, honey," the old, nasty-looking fat lady said, snapping him right out of his zone. "Follow me. She walked over to where Shavon was sitting; she looked at Lil Coon smiling and then left him at Shavon's table.

Finally, Lil Coon looked down at Shavon, who wasn't paying attention. Shavon didn't even know Lil Coon was standing next to her. "Hey, baby, how are you doing? Lil Coon asked, placing his hands on her shoulders; Shavon looked into his eyes and smiled.

Lil Coon took a seat after getting Shavon's attention; the two stared into each other eyes, completely lost on who was staring back at them. For Shavon, she didn't have a common clue about who was sitting across the table from her.

But for Lil Coon, he was trying to figure out if Shavon was who she was supposed to be because the last time he saw her, he didn't know who Shavon was.

"I'ma Barbie girl in a Barbie world... "Come on, Barbie, let's go, Barbie," Shavon started singing like she was on B.E.T. She started snapping her fingers as she sang. All Lil Coon could do was sit back in his chair and look at the woman who stole his heart.

It hurt him so much that it brought tears to his eyes, just looking at the fucked up condition she was in. For the last hour or so, Lil Coon sat there and listened to Shavon sing as she played with the board games.

"Medication time," one of the staff announced over the intercom; Shavon jumped up all happy and shit, clapping her hands. "Medication time," Shavon said as she walked over to where the medication was being served and got in line.

Now Lil Coon knew why Shavon was going crazy; it wasn't a breakdown. It was the medication they had her on. Lil Coon made a mental note in his head to speak with someone about the medicine Shavon was taking, but in the meantime, Lil Coon sat where he was, hoping Shavon would pull through and things would get back to normal again; all he could do was pray and hope for the best.

***

With Shavon in the crazy house, Lil Coon only had one person that he could count on, Myesha. So he decided to let her come through since she went through hell and back for him; it was the very least he could do.

Truth be told, Myesha needed Lil Coon as bad as he needed her; both were heart torn and needed each other. Myesha did what no other woman would do: sacrificing everything, including her life, to show that her loyalty to Lil Coon was real.

Myesha went against the grain and turned against the man she was engaged to. The only reason she was dealing with him was to get back at Lil Coon out of spite. Now that Shavon was in the coo-coo house, she knew this was the time he needed her the most, and if she played her hand right, she'd push Shavon out of the picture for good.

Lil Coon was sitting between Myesha's legs watching 106 & Park and smoking a fat ass blunt; Myesha rubbed Lil Coon's chest and mid area, kissing the side of his neck.

With only socks on Lil Coon's feet and a pair of boxers, everything else was bare. Nothing was on Myesha. She was completely naked. For the last three months, Myesha has been taking dance classes because of the workout that comes with her style of dancing; she loved how it kept her body looking fine.

Lil Coon has not said much since Myesha arrived, nor did he even ask for sex. Myesha knew a lot was on Lil Coon's mind, and she knew what she had to do to get this nigga's mind off Shavon.

Myesha got up from the thick. rugged carpet and started dancing seductively, moving her body like she had been dancing all her life. Lil Coon laid back, putting all his attention on her, watching Myesha as she danced.

For ten minutes, Myesha danced for Lil Coon putting her soul in it, and the way she danced fucked Lil Coon's head up; all the feelings he had once felt for her started to return.

Lil Coon reached to grab Myesha, making her straddle him. "How you feeling, daddy," Myesha asked, putting her arms around his neck,

"I feel much better," Lil Coon responded as he looked into her eyes. "Thanks to you," he said.

That's all Myesha needed to hear! "Take these off," Myesha said, standing up and rubbing her nipples. In less than 3.5 seconds, Lil Coon was standing butt-ass naked with his dick at attention.

Myesha got down on her knees, grabbed Lil Coon's dick, placed it in the warmness of her mouth, and started sucking and licking on it like it was an icy pop. Lil Coon was feeling so relaxed because Myesha's head game was awesome; he let all his stress go putting his energy on the person making him feel good, Myesha.

Because she loved every minute, Myesha started fingering herself until they came at the same time. She tried her best to swallow everything Lil Coon was trying to give her and did so without spilling any of it.

Lay down, Myesha said before climbing on top of him, easing her wet pussy down over Lil Coon's dick. Myesha started riding him, grinding, and bouncing; she fucked him like she was putting a love spell on him.

Myesha fucked Lil Coon for an hour straight before she climbed off his drenched dick. Both of their bodies were soaked from head to toe; there wasn't anything for them to do but cuddle and get some sleep right there on the living room floor.

Nothing Good Lasts Forever
K-Dog
Chapter 31

A private investigator was sitting across from Dominique, ready to reveal what she paid her money for... Facts: Dominique hired a private investigator because it was killing her to know if K-Dog was really cheating.

So, she paid $13,000 to get the right information she needed, and today was the day that the private investigator gave her what she wanted, but deep down in Dominique's heart, she wanted to believe the man she shared vows with wasn't cheating.

"Good evening!" The investigator said, pulling out a big manila envelope.

"Good evening to you, Mr. Sandler," Dominique said, feeling nervous. "This is quite a suite Ms. Williams," said Mr. Sandler admiring her gorgeous, expensive penthouse.

"How much did you spend on something like this?" Mr. Sandler inquired, , looking upset.

"Mr. Sandler, let's just say it was worth it," Dominique said, adjusting her robe. "Now, let's get down to business, shall we?"

Dominique took a sip of coffee as they sat in front of the terrace on the 28th floor, facing Hallandale Beach Ocean. "No problem" let's get right to it." Mr. Sandler reached into his manila envelope, pulling out photos.

Well, Ms. Williams, while I was doing a thorough investigation into your husband, I was able to come up with these" Mr. Sandler passed the photos that were in his hands, giving them to Dominique.

She studied the photos looking at them one at a time. "These photos you are holding are the ones I took, catching your husband in the very act. Dominique looked up at Mr. Sandler for the first time to notice the smirk on his face.

THIS WHITE DEVIL GETS A KICK OUT OF MESSING UP PEOPLE'S LIVES; I BET HE'S DIVORCED OR GAY. WITH HIS DICK TRACY LOOKING ASS. Dominique thought to herself as she sat there totally heartbroken, but she refused to let him see her weak.

Dominique stood up with her head held high, and chest poked out; she went over to her pocketbook, pulling out her check. "Thank you for your time, but your service is no longer needed" Dominique walked over, giving him the check.

"Well thank you." Dominique didn't say a word; she walked over to the door and opened it. Mr. Sandler gathered his things and walked right out the door. BAM! Dominique slammed it shut, placing her back against it, and started crying.

***

K-Dog was sitting at the bar at Club Dungeon enjoying his drink; Cinnamon and Season were sitting on both sides of him. The three of them were dressed like they were going to a fashion show, designer down from head to toe.

Lil Coon had some other chick serving as the bartender instead of Shavon. The baby girl was wearing a black leather skirt with a fish net covering her whole body. K-Dog was staring the woman down, admiring how beautiful she was; he never took his eyes off her, not once, until Lil Coon came out from his office, walking towards K-Dog.

"Wuz up, old timer?" Lil Coon said, giving him a dap.

"Tryna stay above water."

"I can dig it, I can dig it," Lil Coon looked over at both ladies, greeting them. "Dat's Alba," Lil Coon said to K-Dog after noticing what he was looking at.

"Damn, that's a bad bitch, bruh...You were hitting that?"

"Alba, that's my heart," Lil Coon said, looking at how fine she was. "She special, bruh!

"Special, I bet; what in bed or all around?" K-Dog asked

"All ground nigga," Lil Coon responded, making the both laugh. "Look, ya'll have a good time tonight, and don't throw all your money away because you know they have brought it to me," Lil Coon said, giving K-Dog dap.

"Alright, homie; I'll catch you later."

"Bet." Lil Coon walked over to Alba, placing a kiss on her lips before he left the bar and walked back into his office. K-Dog, Cinnamon, and Season were enjoying themselves, smoking and drinking while at the same time throwing a few thousand.

The whole time K-Dog was in the building, he had been trying to text Dominique for the last hour or so, but in return, he received nothing. K-Dog was trying to keep his mind off worrying about Dominique, while at the same time, maintaining his royalty.

K-Dog had both girls dancing for him, Cinnamon, and Season, with a bunch of $1's in one hand and a bottle in the other. Dominique didn't notice Dominique walk into the building until she walked up to him. "Bae wuz up? Wat, you doin here?" K-Dog asked, a little shocked to see her.

"Don't bae me muthafucka what you think I'm fuckin stupid!" Dominique said with her hands on her hips.

"Molly, what the fuck you talking about?" K-Dog said, looking confused.

"About your lil thing, you have with these bitchez.

Dominique looked at Cinnamon and Season. "You thought I wasn't going to find out about them!" Dominique pointed. "How can you do me like this, after all we've been through together?"

Everybody in the club stopped what they were doing to listen to what the fuck was going on; even D.J put the music on pause. "Listen, this is the wrong place and time to talk about this. Can we step outside?"

K-Dog tried to lead her out, but Dominique snatched away from him. "Naw, it ain't shit to talk about; you got caught with your dick in the dirt. Muthafucker, Fuck you"! Dominique yelled as she slapped the shit out of him. Then, she reached into her designer pocketbook, pulled out the photos, and threw them at him, Cinnamon, and Season.

Dominique stormed out that bitch like a bat out of hell, leaving K-Dog with a long face.

***

K-Dog was sitting in his office looking at the photos. Dominique had given him days ago. He couldn't believe Dominique would go this far to hire a private investigator to follow him around and take pictures of him.

That shit didn't sit right with him, but regardless of how he looked at it, he got caught red-handed with his hands in the cookie jar. Dominique wasn't anywhere to be found. It's like she just vanished. Lil Javon and baby girl were at his mom's house, where she had left them weeks ago before disappearing in thin air.

To make matters worse, that would only add fuel to the fire, Dominique had withdrawn all her money out of their shared bank accounts, leaving K-Dog's money. Photos and bank papers were scattered all over his desk as K-Dog added up all the money she took out of their accounts.

Come to find out, Dominique took over $3.7 million, which was all the money she busted her ass for over for many years. Had it been anybody else, they would have taken everything, leaving his ass dry like a well without water.

As for Diamond, she decided to stay at her grandma's house instead of going back home; for some reason, Diamond was mad at her father for what he did to her mother; the strange thing about it was that Diamond was always by her father's side. Daddy's little girl.

K-Dog was feeling out of touch because both of his wonderful precious ladies weren't by his side. Dominique was a ghost, and Diamond didn't want to see his face, and that's what's killing him.

Javon was his Lil Soulja to the end; even though Diamond was his baby girl, Javon will always be his firstborn, and can't anybody take that away from him. K-Dog decided to let Javon stay up past his bedtime because it was the weekend, so he was allowed to play his PS 4 and do whatever he wanted.

K-Dog was sitting on the sofa in the front room watching the first 48 TV shows when his phone started going off. "Hello, he answered on the first ring. "K-Dog, this Percy wuz up?"

"Oh, shit, wuz good with you gangsta...Wuz going on?"K-Dog asked, looking at his Rolex, which read 1:46 am.

"I'm good, homie, I just got in from the laundromat.

"Oh yeah?"

"Yeah, man."

"So how's a business been going for you?" K-Dog asked. "Er'thang gud bruh?" Percy stopped before speaking again."Homie, I need to holler at you? You home?"

"Slide, though. I'm at the crib, bruh!" K-Dog said, sensing something anxious about Percy and besides, Percy never called him that late about anything.

"Aight, I'll be there in a few minutes if it's not a problem with you!" "Problem? Come on, man, you family; you always welcome to my house," K-Dog said, tryna make the best out of the situation.

"Say no more; I'm on my way." Percy ended the call. While K-Dog waited for Percy, he rolled up a big ass blunt to take his mind off Dominique. She was distracting him so that K-Dog didn't see the signs of danger, slapping him right in the face.

Twenty minutes later, a knock came from the front door slapping him right out of his zone. He looked at the camera before getting up and opening the door for Percy. "Wuz good fam" K-Dog reached out, giving him a handshake.

K-Baby wat dey do homie?" Percy said

"Come in nigga, it's cold out this bitch," Percy walked in and waited for K-Dog to lead him to the front room area. Right on the glass front room table was $80,000 in one-hundred-dollar bills sitting there nice and neat.

Percy sat next to K-Dog on the couch, and they both started making small talk while K-Dog rolled another fat ass blunt. Both of their ass chiefing like they were Indians getting higher than the sky. "A K-Dog man, I appreciate erthang you did for me my nigga word up, had it not been for you man, I don't know where I would be?" Percy said, passing the blunt to K-Dog.

"Look, man, I did what was necessary, but you utilized everything. All I did was give you the tools and opportunity to live a better life, and you took it."

"It's a blessing, man, because nobody ever gave me anything, let alone an opportunity to make something of my life," Percy said thanking him.

"God works in mysterious ways."

"Yes, he does," Percy said, standing up and pulling his Fi (gun) from his waistband, cocking it in one motion before pointing it to K-Dog's head.

"Nigga what the fuck you up in my shit pulling a gun on me nigga...you crazy?" K-Dog said, standing up.

Percy took a step back just in case K-Dog wanted to try anything. "I'm sorry, man, I am, but you don't know what I've been going through lately."

"I made a promise."

"A promise!" K-Dog yelled.

"Yeah, nigga a promise," Percy started tripping out, rubbing his head with one hand while he held the gun pointed at K-Dog with the other.

"After all, I did for you, now you telling me about a promise...I...don't... understand." K-Dog didn't know what kind of promise Percy was talking about or what kind of promise Percy made with anybody. Percy had tears in his eyes as he stood in front of K-Dog, not knowing if he could kill the man who killed his father.

"I made a promise to kill the person responsible for killing my father; ever since I didn't follow through, it's been haunting me every night! K-Dog inched where the money was, throwing it in Percy's face. K-Dog grabbed the gun with one hand and used the other to hit Percy in the face repeatedly.

Percy was in trouble, but he knew that if he let K-Dog take his gun from his hands, he would cancel Christmas because he wasn't going to see New Year. Percy held the gun for dear life while K-Dog bashed in his face. Once K-Dog saw he had Percy right where he wanted him, he backed him up until his feet got caught up and fell backward.

Three shots hit K-Dog in the chest area. While Percy lay on his back, K-Dog was on top of him, looking Percy in his eyes. "Karma is a bitch nigga; remember that." These were K-Dog's last words before dropping dead on top of Percy. Percy managed to get the K-Dog's lifeless body off the top of him before emptying the remaining clip in him.

Percy said prayer, opening his eyes only to find J-Money looking at him with pure evil. PAYBACK IS A BITCH... YOU WEEP WHAT YOU SOW...

To be continued... Pt. 3